The Morland Prince

Derek Jensen

edited

(illustrated, clarified, annotated, & generally made
more awesome)

by Peter Lawrence

Cover design by

Hindy

Magic Headaches

Magic Headaches

The Morland Prince

Morland Blood

The Morland Prince

Search

Loading...

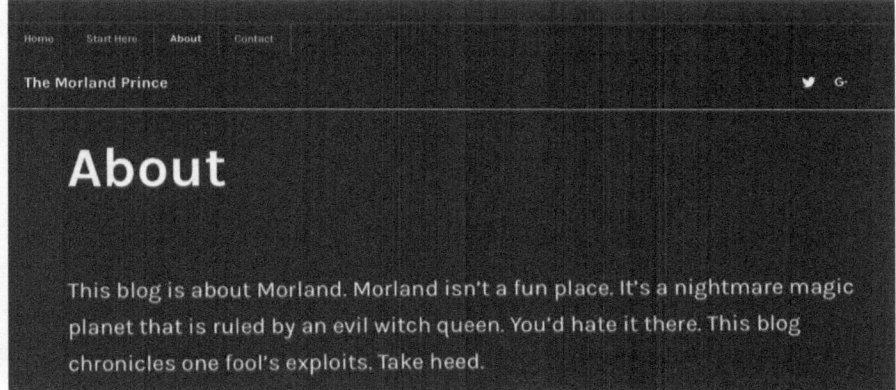

Note from the Editor:

So Derek doesn't know I did this...
   I should probably clarify.

Things Derek doesn't know:

1. That I took his blog and turned it into a book.

2. That I added anything to his story. ie: this but also charts, graphs, illustrations, and snarky comment.

3. That I am sharing his story with ANYONE, especially not with strangers and definitely not with people he might know.

4. How to smile.

5. How to beat me at Magic: The Gathering.
(It's a card game and yes it's as nerdy as you imagine.)
(Did I mention I'm awesome at it?)

Things I don't know:
1. If Derek will ever forgive me.

Note to future Derek:

I'm sorry. I couldn't help myself?

The only changes I've made to Derek's actual blog posts are grammatical changes (probably not for the best, my comma game is weak). His story, as presented here, is just what you'd find in his blog, The Morland Prince.

Everything I've added will be in my handwriting, like this.

You'll see as you read on, but Derek's story has a way of consuming you. It's like it takes root in your brain, like an alien or something.

But like I said to future Derek, I couldn't help myself. I know I'm supposed to hate Morland. I mean Derek HATES it soooo much but Morland fascinates me. And I can't let it go.

So I made this. Whatever this is. A stalker's secret notebook? A fanboy's encyclopedia? No, a travel guide for your upcoming trip to... Your worst nightmare.

Look to your left to see the Darkness.

Notice how it taints everything

And to the right you'll see the fire witch queen. Don't get too close. Ha ha but really. Watch yourself.

Welcome, I guess...

Not sure how you found your way here. And I'm not sure what I'm supposed to say to you now. It's good you are here. You need to read this. Everyone does. Not that it's the greatest story ever written but it's true and it's mine and you need to know what could happen to you. People always say "What's the worst thing that could happen?"

And the answer is THIS.

This is the worst thing that could happen to you. So study up. I know it would have been a million times easier if I'd read a story by someone who'd walked the path before me. But I carve my own stupid path. No one else would take the lonely path lined in blood and darkness.

Good luck, I guess.

So kind of gloomy huh?
This is how he introduces his readers to his blog.
shakes head
Derek is not known for his optimism.

How Derek sees life   How life really is

9

Before

My life is very clearly demarcated by a before and its after. Most people's lives aren't like that; I've found. Most people's befores and afters are a smudgy business, blurry guesses containing many small events that lead a winding path from the land of before to the nightmare of after. My before is written in **bold**. It's spelled out in fireworks. It's a crack that spans my whole world.

I write this because I have to, because the weight of it hangs like an anchor around my neck. I know this won't help. I know it doesn't change anything but maybe I'll sleep a little better. And I haven't had a good night's sleep in so many years. Maybe the people who read this will remember the missteps I took if their fates lie along a similar path to mine. I wouldn't wish my past on my worst enemy.

Well, actually I would.

I would wish it on *her*. I'd wish what happened to me times a thousand over on her. I guess that makes me a monster but I already know that. And it's good that you learn it now. It will help you not feel sorry for me when you read what's coming.

Hello, my name is Derek and I'm a soulless murdering monster.

If this were a support group, it would be your line to say "Hello, Derek."

But you wouldn't want to know me without the safety of these pages to separate us. Enjoy the story. I hope you don't have too many nightmares. I know I still do. Ten years seems like a long time ago but nightmares have a way of staying fresh in the mind, don't they?

Hello, my name is

Derek

soulless murdering
monster

He's not sooo bad. Most of the time.
Sometimes. It's, uh, complicated?

Hello, my name is

Peter

best friend

Don't think about what kind of person is
best friends with a murderer.
Move past it.

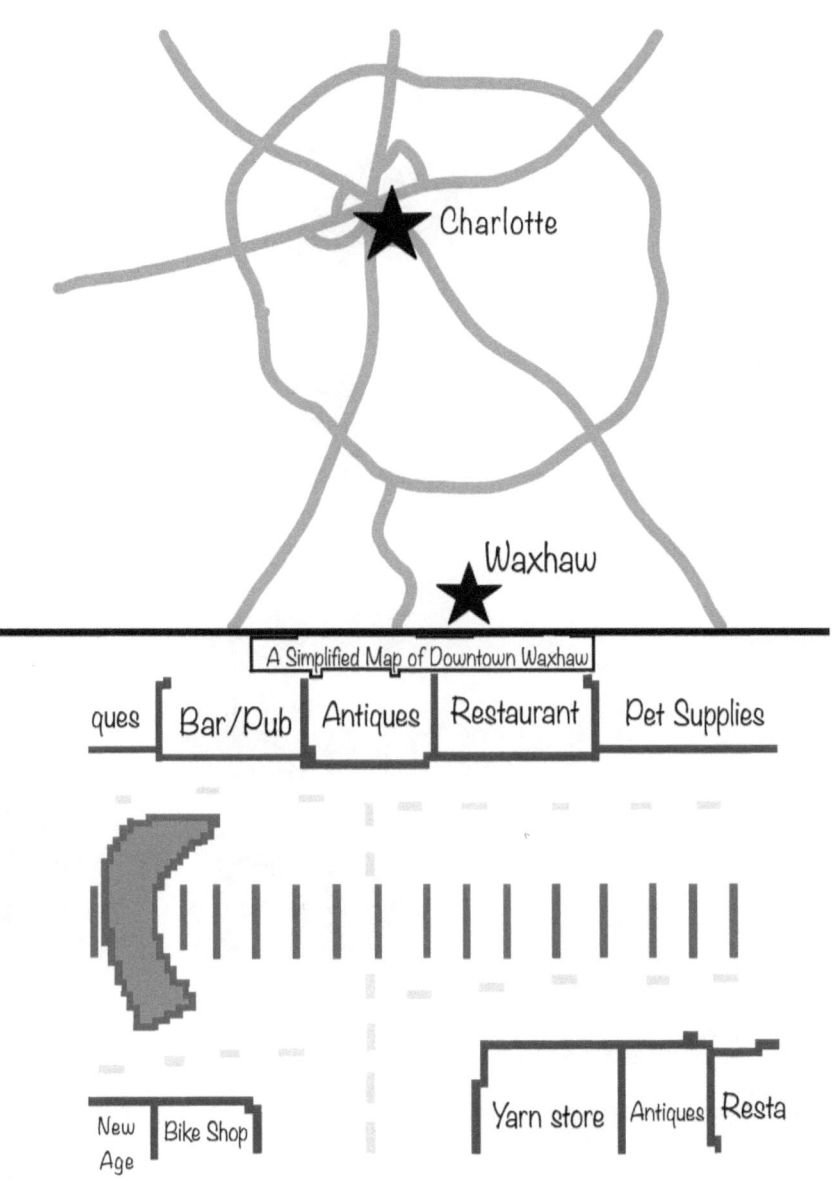

Charlotte

Waxhaw

A Simplified Map of Downtown Waxhaw

ques | Bar/Pub | Antiques | Restaurant | Pet Supplies

New Age | Bike Shop

Yarn store | Antiques | Resta

Worse Than a Rabbit Hole

1

Waxhaw, North Carolina is almost asleep. That's one of the best things about it. It's easy to pretend that nothing *has ever* happened and that nothing *will ever* happen.

There is the usual bloody history of settlers killing the natives and there was a president who was born here. But besides that it's quintessentially a small town. People visiting call it 'quaint' and 'adorable' with its train running through downtown and its excessive number of pet accessory stores. But then they also complain about how far away it is from everything. There is a Target now and more restaurants close by but it still feels like it's in the middle of nowhere, which is exactly why I like it.

I was born here, not in the house I live in now but not far. I'm an only child, well, kind of. I'll get to that later. I am *my parents'* only child and I wonder if things would have been different if I'd grown up with a sibling, a brother to smack some sense into me or a sister... But it was good enough, for a while. My folks both worked a lot and I played a lot of video games and ate a lot of pizza rolls. I was living the dream. But I had an itch, this weird restlessness, that drove me outside.

Oh, what a dumb fool.

I've thought a lot about time travel. I know the basic theories floating around and I've watched a lot of Doctor Who. And I wonder if what happened to me could be *undone*. There is a theory that there are fixed points, moments in history that are essential to the structure of the future. If those moments were undone, the future would break and crumble and all of time would be destroyed. What happened to me couldn't be a fixed point. It was a careless mistake, bad luck.

So yeah, I've looked into it. Time travel, I mean. But it's really not as easy as you'd think. And I'm not as clever as I wish. I'm clever in a get-out-of a-trap-before-the-axe-comes-down-to-chop-my-head-off kind of way but not clever in an advanced-calculus-string-theory-physics kind of way. But if I could figure it out, I know just the moment I'd go back to.

It was early summer. I had just turned thirteen. I'd slept till noon and was eating half my weight in cheese puffs and I got that itch again. If I had a time machine, I'd go back to that moment. I'd go into the garage to get some rope, lighter fluid, matches and an axe. I'd go inside and tie the young me to a chair. It would be very easy. He was all gangly limbs and no muscle.

Then I'd go into the woods behind my house and cut down

Every. Bloody. Tree.

I've thought about how satisfying that would be. I know it's a weird fantasy, chopping down trees, but I get a little giddy imagining it. I'd chop them down to kindling. My arms would be sore but I'd love every bleeding stroke. I'd pile it all together and soak it in lighter fluid. (I'd probably need the gasoline from the lawnmower as well.) Once it was soaked and I was getting a little high off the fumes, I'd toss the match. It would knock me back but I'd walk right back over and watch it burn.

Oh, that would be sweet.

I could do all this now. I know that and I've thought about it. But doing it now doesn't change anything. I've rested the axe at the base of a tree once or twice and I couldn't do it. I'm not afraid... but I still don't do it. Because it would only mean something if I could do it *then,* before it all broke.

2

It started with a tree. It started with a walk in the woods. I've thought about this day a million times if I've thought about it once. I was sure that if could just remember everything then I'd be able to find the secret to getting home. I don't know if it was fate or destiny or just the worst luck of all time that led *me* to *that* tree.

I was a restless teenager, only just thirteen like I said. And I needed to get out of my stifling empty house, away from everything. My parents were working late, again. I felt agitated and angry and thought that being up in a tree might make it easier to breathe. The forest behind my house was large and it took a couple minutes to find a suitable tree. It had an appealing y-shape that looked like it would make a cozy seat for being free.

Even though I was alone, I was still a thirteen-year-old boy and needed to run up the tree as cool as possible. There was a good-looking foothold most of the way up the tree. I thought if I could make it to that, I could propel myself up in one jump.

That is not what happened.

My foot slipped. I tumbled over myself and banged my head on a branch. I woke up later with blurred vision and blood-matted hair. I was hanging with half of my body on each side of the tree's y. Below me, in broken pieces, was the branch that had tried its best to make its way into my brain.

While trying to right myself, I fell forward and down headfirst. More lost time. When I next awoke, I was waiting for my eyes to focus and my head to stop spinning. My vision wasn't so much blurry as faded, like everything was duller and browner somehow. I was obviously not well. I needed to go home. I forced myself up and started walking back the way I had come. I was pretty sure I had a concussion.

It took about fifteen minutes before I became concerned. I should have been home already. The woods behind my house were big but not big enough to get lost in. And behind the trees was a field that grew corn sometimes. But the more I walked, all I saw were trees and more trees.

I also couldn't find my phone anywhere. I checked my pockets but when I looked down I realized I wasn't wearing *my* pants.

This is a weird realization to have.

I had been wearing jeans when I'd left the house that afternoon. Now I was wearing some kind of dark brown linen pants and a shirt of the same fabric but in a lighter color.

This. Freaked. Me. Out.

It was some horrible hallucination, I was sure. I felt the back of my head and it wasn't bleeding anymore but it didn't feel pretty either. It hurt enough when I touched it to make me instantly nauseous.

I knew from medical T.V. shows that when you get a concussion you were supposed to stay awake but the tiredness was pulling at me like a giant anchor and the strangeness of the day had me exhausted and freaked out, so I slept.

Morning came and my situation had not changed. I walked around trying to find my way back home. On the third day while I stumbled towards a clearing, I was knocked to the ground from behind. I looked up stunned to see a man holding a sword which he pointed at my face. He pulled out an old fashioned pair of shackles and bound me before I could object. This was the beginning on my tumble into darkness.

Math Lesson

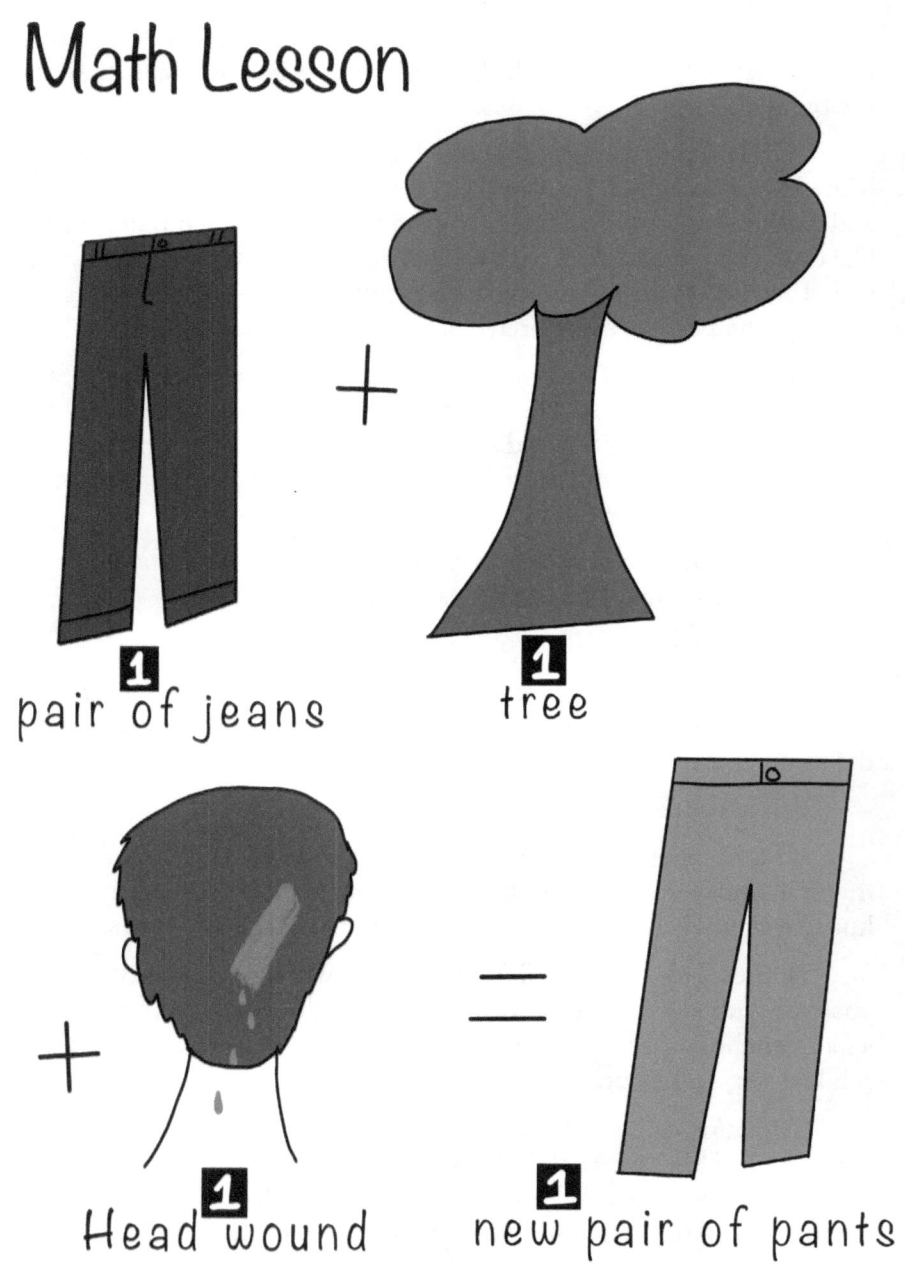

1 pair of jeans

1 tree

1 Head wound

1 new pair of pants

The Mage

1

I'd been captured since the early morning and my three captors had been silently pulling me along all day. The iron shackles were *not* as fun as the movies made them look. I'd complained at first but the gray haired man, Jol, had slapped me. Hard. And then told me to shut up.

I found out halfway through the trip that they thought I was a thief. Someone my age had stolen something from someone. It took me too long to figure that out and by then my protestations of innocence were not believed. My speaking up was quickly met with a slap or a kick.

I amazingly still hadn't grasped that I wasn't 'in Kansas anymore'. We finally stopped walking when the sun set. I felt so dazed and my head pounded. When Jol walked past I spoke up. I didn't care if he hit me again. I had to make someone believe me. I hadn't eaten in days. I was starving and I needed a doctor. And I missed my parents.

"You've got the wrong guy," I said. "I didn't steal anything. You should just let me go. My parents will be looking for me."

Jol paused and sneered, "And who are your parents that we should care? Will they repay what you have stolen?" His accent was English, British English. *Weird.* Waxhaw was in the south. I'd never met anyone with an accent that wasn't southern. Let alone a British accent.

"My parents are Jenny and Nathan Jensen. My dad is a lawyer at a firm in Charlotte. I'm sure we could sort out whatever misunderstanding this is."

Jol really stared me down before he spoke. Like he was thinking about something. Like he was trying to see through me...

"Where was that? Southtown, did you say?" he said leaning closer until we were only a foot apart.

"Where? No, Charlotte. I don't know what kind of LARPing group this is but I'm not into dressing up and pretending I'm an elf or whatever you guys are doing. I just want to go home. I hit my head pretty hard," I said touching the back of my head and pulling back blood I showed it to him as evidence. He stared at me for a long moment. Staring seemed to be his thing.

His eyes could be so calculating without moving a millimeter, like his internal calculations were too fast for the regular human eye to notice. He didn't say anything but he went to talk to one of the other men who shrugged and then headed the other direction.

"They are taking their dinner now," Jol said. "I'm not as weak as I look." He raised is eyebrows as if daring me to try something. He was about sixty maybe older, gray haired, but no worse from the wear. He was strong and he looked like he knew his way around the sword he was carrying. There was something about his stance that made me wary to test him and my hands were still chained up anyway.

"What are you doing in these woods if you aren't the thief we are looking for?" he asked uninterested, as he sat down and stretched from the long day.

"I got lost."

He barked a laugh and looked at me levelly. "You are a long way from anywhere. Only people in trouble hide out in these woods."

"It can't be that far. I'm probably only a couple miles from my house, well before I was dragged to wherever we are now."

"Where were you born?" he asked surprising me.

"Waxhaw, North Carolina."

"And where do you think you are?" he asked

"Um, like I said, a couple miles from my house in Waxhaw, I guess."

"I think you hit your head harder than you know. I've never heard of these places," he said looking me up and down. "How did you get so lost?"

"I was in my backyard going for a walk and I went to climb a tree. But I hit my head somehow and after a couple days you guys found me. Can you just take me home?"

"A tree?" Jol asked ignoring my request. "In a meadow?"

"No, in the forest behind my house. Please I just want to go home. I didn't steal anything from you guys. I swear!"

"You are farther from your house than you could possibly realize."

Jol tapped his fist on his chin, thinking. The sun had just finished setting and he reached his right hand over the ground and flicked his wrists. A small fire blazed out of nothing and stayed burning in his hand.

I jumped back but didn't get far. He didn't say anything but he moved his gaze skyward and I saw it. The moon. It was gold.

Not a harvest moon or a blood moon, liked I'd seen before. And I'd know my moon anywhere. Everything about this moon was alien. The craters looked wrong and the color could only be called a shimmering gold. And looking around I realized that what I'd assumed was poor light or pollution was just the real color of things. Everything was sepia and everything was different.

"Where am I?" I said turning to Jol in despair.

"Morland."

2

Morland. That word. It changed everything. I felt a rush of excitement I didn't understand.

"What?" I said. "Where is that?"

"It's the smallest planet in the Chrome solar system," he told me.

Okay let's pause here for a moment. Now he could have said 'It's the planet we live on, stupid' or he could have said that we were in the South Woods, which would have been a more reasonable answer.

If someone came up to me in Waxhaw after looking at the moon in abject horror and asked me where he was, I would not say 'Earth'. It was such an obvious thing. I would say, "Hello crazy person, you are in Waxhaw." I might even add the North Carolina part but I would never think to say "You are on the planet Earth, the third rock from the sun," Just like if someone asked what day it was I wouldn't give them the year. I'd just say that it was Tuesday the fifth or whatever.

So that should have tipped me off that he might be hiding something, that he knew something. But I really only remembered all of that conversation recently. It's too late to ask him, thank god. But it's weird, right? Why would he think to tell me that we were on Morland?

That means that he thought I might be from another planet. It's just another weird puzzle piece that I'll never know the answer to but it's really okay. It doesn't keep me up. There are real things that keep me from sleep, worse things.

3

Jol somehow convinced the other men that I wasn't their perp but he was still going to take me with him for further questioning. It wouldn't have been hard to convince them. He was *the* Mage. I didn't know at the time what that meant but oh I'd learn. Jol could pretty much do whatever he liked and he did. I followed him and peppered him with questions that he ignored or growled at.

"Enough!" he said after I'd asked him how he did his magic and if I could have magic and when I could go home and when we were having lunch and if it could be something better than jerky, hard cheese and that horrible tea and when I could get an awesome cloak like his.

He finally roared, "I should have left you to rot in prison!" (He probably should have.)

"Can you shut up for five minutes?" (It appeared that I couldn't.)

But he was stuck with me, for a while at least. We ended our traveling in the town of Olton where Jol's house was. It was a day's journey from the castle and Jol's house was just far enough from the beaten path that it seemed we were a thousand miles from anywhere.

"I'm bringing a physician to the house. How is your accent?" Jol asked handing me a cup of tea. I reached for it reluctantly. I'd grown up in the land of *cold* sweet tea and had never been a fan of hot tea. And Jol's tea was like burning hot dirt and sludge. I've since had a million cups of tea and thankfully all Morland tea isn't bad. It's just Jol's ability to turn anything into a bitter, scummy version of itself.

"I don't know. How's this?" I asked in a horrible mix between country and British. My own ears cringed at the sound.

"Unbelievable! I told you to fix this the *day* we met and yet after all of our days traveling you somehow sound worse. You have no idea what will happen to you if you are singled out. If word gets out that you are different you will be sent to the Queen. Do you want her to learn that you aren't from Morland? Do you want her to find a way back to your world?"

I shook my head but his threat meant nothing to me. I didn't know anything about the Queen or Morland. I just wanted to go home and I would follow his rules until then.

"I'll give you one week to learn. One week you will be allowed to stay in my house. Not an hour more. Practice like your life depends on it because it does. And do not speak to the physician. I'll be back."

I kept my mouth shut for the doc. He gave me some medicine and he bound my head up with bandages soaked in strong smelling herbs. Apparently I was not going to die but he wanted me to rest for a couple days. Jol had no intention of being my nurse so he stocked the house with food and water and said he'd be back in a couple days.

"Where are you going?" I asked afraid to see him go. What if he didn't come back?

"To figure out what to do with you!" Jol said rolling his eyes. He loved to roll his eyes, almost as much as he enjoyed furrowing his eyebrows. And they were glorious eyebrows.

Turned out that Jol's plan for my life was to sell me to the army. He didn't call it that but that's what he did. I was honestly a little old to join up. They took kids when they were ten or so. But Jol was the Mage and did whatever he bloody well wanted. (See I eventually learned the accent.)

4

I might should have started with this but I know almost nothing about Jol. I don't think he ever married or has any kids. I don't think he has anyone or anything. He was "The Mage" and nothing else.

But that was something.

There are only two magic wielders alive on Morland or only two that are allowed to live: the Queen and Jol. They both have fire magic. Was Jol the Queen's hound or champion or slave? I didn't know. Did he serve her willingly? Had he ever stood against her? Yes, just the once and it was enough. Or more than once. He kept my secret from her.

He *could* have been a good friend. But I was an impossible brat who grew into a murdering monster and Jol was an ice cold assassin who turned into ... Well he didn't actually evolve but maybe his evil was already peaked by the time I knew him so there was nowhere to go.

Because one thing you need to know about Jol is that he isn't the hero. He also isn't the mentor or teacher like every coming of age novel says he should be. Jol is more like an opportunistic mercenary whose fee was his own life. I don't know why I ruminate on Jol so much.

This chapter of my life is over forever. I'll never see Jol again and I'll never see Morland again. And I wish that that knowledge would free me from remembering it all. Free me from obsessing. Because the truth is that even if I somehow discovered everything there was so know about Jol, it would change nothing and it would do nothing. Because what happened, happened. And Jol was a big part of it.

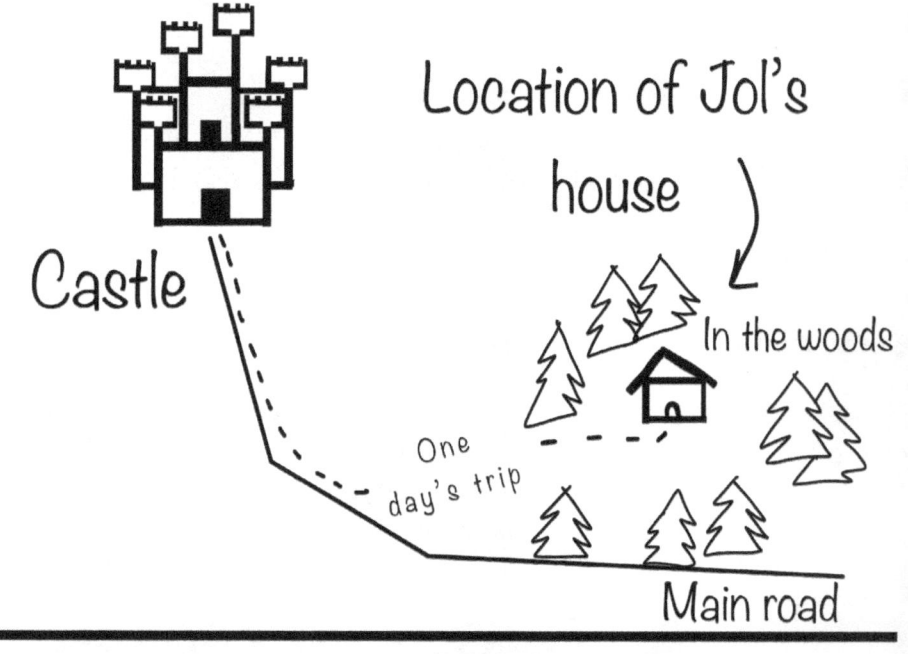

Location of Jol's house

Castle

In the woods

One day's trip

Main road

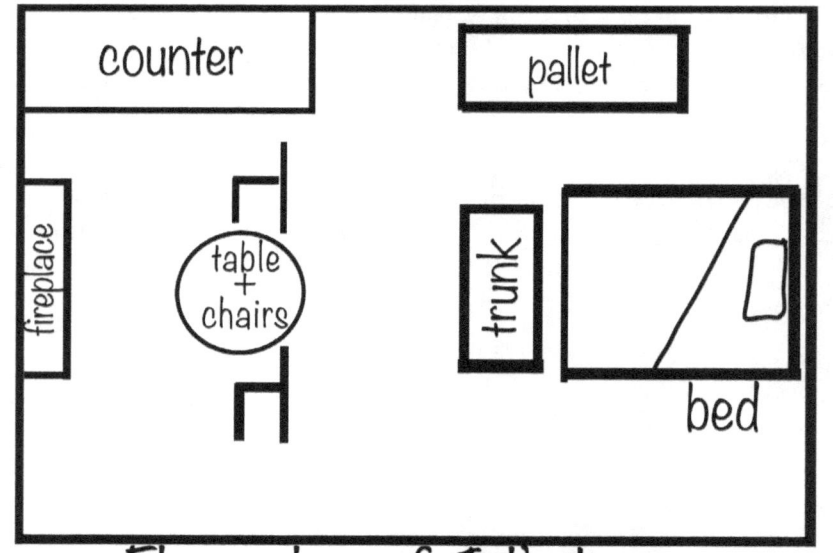

counter

pallet

fireplace

table + chairs

trunk

bed

Floor plan of Jol's house

26

My Soul

1

If I had been asked before, I would have said that, of course, I would notice if I lost my soul. How could someone not know they had lost the part of themselves that was immortal, that was their compass for truth? But it took me *days*. In my defense I did end up having a serious concussion from the tree incident. Looking back, I knew I felt off but I thought that was all it was. So much was happening around me and I was so confused. It was strange that losing my soul wasn't the biggest thing that was going on.

Jol's house was plain and utilitarian. It had a kitchen and a bedroom/living area. He must have been getting paid well but he chose to live in simplicity to the point of scarcity. I've had a lot of key moments in life that happened in Jol's house but the first one was when I saw *him* for the first time. Jol was off on his mission to figure out what to do with me. So I was thankfully alone or alone-ish. I was sitting on one of Jol's two chairs when a voice from behind me startled me from my boredom.

"There you are, you big dummy."

I yelled falling out of the chair and felt myself go pale. I was looking at *myself*. Not a reflection in the mirror but a walking, talking doppelgänger of myself. Except the version across from me had a sword at his waist and I did not.

"Who are you?" I stammered out, pressing myself against the wall. He just looked at me. "Are you a ghost?" I asked stupidly. (This question will continue to make him laugh for many years.)

"You don't know who I am?" he asked chuckling. "A ghost?" He laughed again. "You are so stupid. I'll give you another guess." He nodded towards me encouragingly. I had nothing to say. I had no guess.

He was my twin and it was very bizarre to be talking to a guy who looked and sounded just like me. Did I have a twin? Was there a version of me that existed in Morland? Anything was possible at this point.

"Okay. Let's calm down and take a seat," he said noticing my silence and deer-in-the-headlights look. He sat down in front of me with his legs crossed. He nodded his head down indicating I was to do the same. I tentatively copied him. Was he a copy of me? A clone?

"What do you think happened at the tree?" he asked me.

This was a question I could answer. I had thought a lot about the tree and how I could have possibly ended up in Morland by climbing it.

"I climbed it and somehow hit my head. I must have been hanging unconscious for a while before I woke up and then fell on my head. Then I woke up on the ground and wandered around for a long time before Jol found me."

"Yes. Good. But how long where you just lying there with half your body on each side of the tree before you fell down? A while. That's what pulled me out. I got ripped away from you and sent here..." he said passing his hand though the chair's leg as if it didn't exist. Or as if he didn't exist. "I'd thought you would have noticed I was gone..." he said looking a little hurt.

"What are you talking about?" I asked.

"Nothing yet?" he asked looking at me. "Okay, slowpoke. Now let's do an experiment. Think of something bad that you've done. Something recent. Something you feel bad about."

I did. I thought of the bird I'd accidentally killed with my slingshot last month. I'd felt really bad. I'd only been messing around and I'd killed it. But when I recalled the story something was different. I remembered that I'd felt bad at the time but I didn't now. It felt like it had happened to someone else.

"The bird, right?" he asked. "Do you feel bad?" I shook my head.

"Well I certainly do. I'm your soul, you idiot. Can't you tell?" he asked.

"What?" I said just staring at the boy who looked like me. "I think I'm seeing things from hitting my head. This is not real," I repeated it to myself a couple times as a mantra. "This is not real. This is not real."

"Uh. It's really insufferable seeing us from the outside. I'm your soul. You know it's true. You'd be able to feel it, if you thought about it for more than like a second. When we fell through the tree, we were transported here to Morland. It must have been some kind of portal.

"When we got stuck half in half out, I got yanked free from you. I knew what had happened but I felt all hazy and insubstantial. It took me a while to find you when I came to. I can kind of feel where you are. No one else can see me. Believe me I've tried."

"This is really strange," I told myself out loud. But as strange and impossible as it was to be sitting across from my soul having a chat, I knew it was actually happening. I felt it. It was true. "This is so weird."

"Maybe for you, I guess. I've always known I existed. But you never really have. Well, surprise, you have a soul! I'm just unfortunately on the outside now. But think of the plus, you now have one friend in this dumb new world."

"How come you have a sword," I asked him. It didn't seem fair that he had one and I didn't. "Did you find it somewhere?"

"Nope. It was just here," he said taking it out of its holder. "I just had it when I woke up. It's cool. Sorry you didn't get one, too."

Once I knew how to recognize it, it was so obvious that I'd been split in two. I didn't feel things the same way. I didn't see things the same way.

On my own I was meaner and coarser. But when he was near, it was like I remembered how to be a good person. It was still a choice like it had always been but now I had an actual representation of the angel on my shoulder. He appeared to be all the good that had been in me. He wasn't perfect but then I'd never been. He was just all the best parts of me and I was stuck being someone even I didn't really like.

Morland has played a lot of jokes on me and dealt me a ton of crappy hands but this one thing almost made for it. Having my soul as my constant companion was a gift. Jol came back that evening and I decided not to tell him. I didn't know if he'd believe me and I think it was starting to sink in that Jol wasn't my friend. He informed me that the next day I would start my new life as a solider in the Queen's army. It was really for the best that I didn't feel things as strongly anymore. There was a lot of bloodshed ahead of me and it almost seemed like my soul was removed from all the things I was doing. Maybe just one part of myself wouldn't be ruined.

Portal Magic

Things we know:

1. In Waxhaw, NC there is (inexplicably) a portal to another planet. Portal is between the branches of a random tree.

2. Getting stuck half in and half out is a very bad thing.

Pulls your soul out.

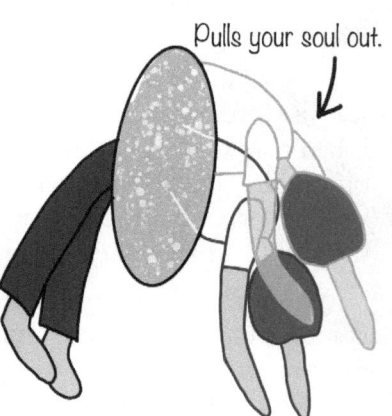

3. Item conversion... Earth things don't pass through but are kindly replaced with Morland equivalent items. But why does the souls get the sword? And what was the sword replacing? Cell phone?

6

2

I'm sure that everyone has conversations that they replay over and over in their minds. There are few conversations I replayed more than this one. I'd think on it for hours, making sure I'd heard what I'd heard and hoping by some miracle that there was more to remember. And the stupidest thing about this at that it wasn't really a conversation.

It was the first night my soul was with me at Jol's house. Despite my head having stopped bleeding and the physician assuring me I would soon be 'good as new', I didn't feel 'good' or 'new' yet. Probably just my soul being gone or on the outside.

"Good. You are still awake," Jol said looking over as he closed the door behind himself and removed his cloak. "Tomorrow, early, we'll head to the city. I've enlisted you at the Citadel."

"What is that? Like a school or something? The Citadel," I said testing it out. "Am I going to a magic school?"

My soul was grinning ear to ear. And then my soul said for the first and last time, "Maybe Morland isn't the worst." Jol followed my gaze but I turned back to him. It was strange that he couldn't see my soul.

"No, idiot," he growled. "Haven't I told you that the Queen and myself are the only mages on Morland. Do you think that is a lucky accident? Pray to whatever god you believe in that there is no magic in your blood. No, the Citadel is the headquarters and training center for the Queen's army. You start tomorrow."

"Army? I'm just a kid. I'm only thirteen. There has got to be something else I could do. I could be your apprentice or your assistant or something. Or I could learn leather working or some other trade. I don't want to be a solider."

Jol sighed angrily and slammed his fists on the table.

"Who do you think I am? Do you think I explore the woods looking for foundling boys to raise as my own? I am one of the most important men on this planet. You should be in prison but I listened to your stupid story. I have taken you into my home. And you are the most ungrateful child I have ever met. It was no easy task to convince the General to allow you to enlist. Most are children when they enter the Citadel. You are six years too old and six years behind. It will be a miracle if it doesn't kill you. I was doing you a favor by enlisting you. Otherwise you would become a beggar on the streets. What skills do you have? What master craftsman would want such a stupid ignorant boy?"

"Jol, hey that's not," I started to argue but Jol's growl silenced me.

"If you want to live until tomorrow you will never speak without the proper accent again. I am tired of warning you. Are you capable? Should I just kill you now? Can you not learn this one thing?"

I nodded. I'd been doing well the past couple days but in my anger I'd slipped up.

"If you listen to nothing I have said listen to this: You do not want to stand out. You do not want people to try to figure out what's different about you. You do not want to draw attention. Learn to look, walk, act, and speak like everyone else. Learn to be invisible and you'll live."

"For how long?" I asked and he nodded at my enunciation.

"Forever. Forever, Derek. I thought you understood... There is no going home," Jol said speaking without anger for the first time in a while.

"I..." I started to say but what was there to say. I sat down on the edge of the bed and stared at the ground. I was never going home. Jol was silent but my soul got down in front of me and made me look at him.

"He's wrong. He's wrong, Derek. He's just a man. He doesn't know everything. He doesn't know anything about Earth. He doesn't know anything about the portal we took to get here. We just have to find it again. That's our mission. Live long enough to find the way home. Don't give up hope. We'll master the accent. I'll help you," he said stuttering into a British accent. "One step at a time, okay. We've got the facts and now we can make a plan. We'll face tomorrow first and then we'll go from there."

I nodded and Jol went outside to get firewood and start dinner. We ate a meal of stew and bread that he must have purchased in the city. One good thing about leaving Jol was that I wouldn't have to eat his cooking anymore.

The conversation that I've memorized happened later when Jol thought I was asleep. He'd given me a pallet on the floor but even late into the evening he still hadn't gone to bed. I was getting irritated because if he wasn't going to sleep, at least he could have given me the bed instead of a blanket on the floor. Typical Jol.

He was sitting by the fire drinking his fourth cup of his vile tea. I wasn't trying to spy on him or eavesdrop or anything. I had wanted to

32

get lots of sleep but I was nervous about the morning and the floor was really hard.

He started muttering to himself and at first I thought it was just the fire crackling. My soul sat up straight. He had been lying down beside me even though he told me that he couldn't actually sleep. We both strained our ears to see if we could hear what Jol was saying. My soul walked over but I stayed still pretending to be asleep.

"You are a fool, old man," Jol said taking a deep sip from his mug. "I can't believe I've gotten myself in such a dangerous situation. I never would have believed I would do this if I hadn't watched as it all happened," Jol sighed and massaged his forehead with his free hand. "What now? Good heavens, what now?"

Jol was silent for a while and I started to fall asleep for real. Jol extinguished the fire and exhaled a deep breath. Then he said it. "What do I care what happens to this boy? His fate is his own. But maybe... no. It's not worth it. And it would probably never work."

Then Jol went to bed.

'It would probably never work'. *What* would probably never work?

3

I missed home like crazy at first. That was before I figured out how to cure the homesickness. The trick, in case you ever find yourself trapped in a hellish Morland-esque situation, is to lie to yourself and to forget everything good that has ever happened. It seems simple, I know. But it's not. So I'll walk you through it.

1. Lie to yourself.

It's a lot of little things that you have to lie about. You have to transform your memories of truth. Truth is not, for instance, that your parents are really great people who have always loved and cared for you. You can't think that, it'll kill you. So instead your new truth is "My parents are so self-absorbed in their lives that they probably don't even know I'm gone."

Another truth you need to accept is that you are never going home. Even accepting this truth doesn't mean you stop looking for the way, it couldn't stop me. But you stop expecting anyone to save you or anything good to happen to magically send you home. You'll still look for the way because Morland is so horrible you'd kill yourself if this was all there was. But you'll know deep down that you are never going home. It'll stop stinging so much. Eventually.

That last lie leads into the second trick, your home, your old life was crap. The only things you are allowed to remember are the worst things. Your folks yelling at you, your dog getting run over by a car on Christmas, your best friend saying that he hated you after you got the spot of the baseball team. Little gems like those are amazing tonics for homesickness. Because why miss a thing when it might actually be worse than where you are now.

2. Forget everything good that ever happened. This is critical. Everything that doesn't fit into the category "Worst Things" has to be erased from your mind. You can't think about video games, or the internet, or your mother holding you after a bad day at school, or god forbid, don't think of McDonalds. Purge your mind of everything except your name. It helps if you can absolutely exhaust yourself every day. It's so much easier to forget your old life when you are too tired to even take off your own shoes.

3. If at all possible, have your soul outside your body. I know that most things I feel are muted, except rage. I get that in spades. Everything else though... It's like pulling an anchor through quicksand.

So as hard as it was to be away from home, I know it could have been worse. I don't know what my soul feels. But I know he feels sad ten times more than I do. I'm really grateful for it, for the reduced feeling capacity but also for the friend. That's the real reason to pull your soul from your body, if you can, you'll always got someone to talk to. Except when he goes off on his own and is gone for really important moments that shape and ruin the rest of your life. I know I'm not selling this well but really I'm so glad he is on the outside.

Castle
Citadel
Shops
+
Homes

Layout of Capital

Hezekiah

1

I was unprepared for everything Morland had to throw at me. I had no skills and no knowledge both of which had to be painfully rectified over time. The Citadel was the center of Morland's military forces. A good portion of the area was used for training. I was placed with the new recruits who, unlike myself, were a bunch of ten-year-olds. At first I'd been irritated to be placed with the young kids but as the day progressed I'd wished there was an easier class I could have been downgraded to.

I was so far behind the youngest class and I felt like an imbecile. We started the day by running as fast as we could for two hours on the track surrounding the Citadel. The slowest, me, got whipped. Then we did hours of sword stances, one pose after another. The worst, me, got whipped. Then we ran again, more whipping and at the end of the day we lifted weights, a.k.a unloaded the shipments of wine, food, and equipment into the storehouse. By the end of the first day, I had a black eye, five lash marks on my back, and I'd thrown up twice.

Maybe it doesn't sound terrible but there was a lot of whipping in-between those steps and it was a huge change from my mostly sedentary lifestyle. I was falling apart. I will never understand how whipping someone is supposed to make them better at doing a thing. They do it in movies all the time. It is a punishment that is supposed to make the slave or solider stop slacking off. But I wasn't slacking off. I was doing my best and it was killing me and I wasn't a third good enough.

My soul was having a hard time as well or so he told me. But really it's worse to be the one being beaten then the one who has to watch helplessly. It has to be worse. At first he stayed close and cheered me on but it was very distracting because I kept turning my head to look at someone who was invisible to everyone but me.

That first night, as I lay in agony on a thin mat in a bunkhouse with a dozen strangers, my soul came to talk. It sounded like most people were asleep but we both whispered anyway.

"I'm sorry, Derek," my soul said.

"I'm pretty sure none of this is your fault. Well except for distracting me. You've got to make yourself scarce. I can't keep turning to look for you when it's taking everything I have just to walk."

"I'm sorry. I'll be better tomorrow. But what if there is something I have to tell you or something you have to tell me. We need a signal."

"That's actually not a stupid idea. You can spy around the Citadel. You need to find a way to escape this nightmare. Better to live in the forest. We read Robinson Crusoe. We can figure it out. Anything has to be better than this. And this was only the first day!"

"Okay. I can do that. I'll find something. We'll get out of here. How about we make this our signal?" He whistled five sharp notes. I wanted to repeat it back to him to make sure I could do it but there was no way to whisper a whistle.

"Deal," I said. "But be quiet now. I *have* to get to sleep."

As the first week went on I was in no better shape. My body was not adapting quick enough and I really was afraid I'd die.

"What have you found?" I asked my soul at the end of the sixth day. I was too exhausted to even sit up so I just laid there and whispered. "You must have found something, right?"

My soul sat on the floor by my head and I felt pretty certain that looking at him was not like looking in a mirror anymore. He was still clean and unblemished while I was one big bruise covered in dirt and blood. I'd see him sometimes practicing along with us using his sword but he never got sweaty or dirty or beaten.

"Umm. Okay so I've really looked around. Everywhere and... there is no way out. They are itching for someone to try and run away. There are eight exits: four go into the castle and four go into town. And each is guarded by two men. No one comes or goes without identification."

"What about alleys or going out of windows?"

"Not gonna work. I don't know how much you noticed about the city when you arrived but it's built in rings surrounding the castle. Castle in the middle. Then the Citadel circling around. Then the city proper circling that.

"The Citadel itself is basically a sandwich with barracks and rooms on the inner and outer wall and open sparing areas in between. There are four doors that lead from the inner walls into the castle ground and four doors that lead from the outer walls into the city proper with shops and housing.

"There are a lot of people in the city. If we could escape, then we'd be able to hide pretty easily but it would be hard to get out of the city. The guards would be looking for us and we'd have to hide long enough for your face to heal. I don't think anyone would take us in so that would mean living on the street for a week or so. Which is doable but... We aren't getting out of the Citadel through any of the doors and there are no windows to climb through. The roof of the Citadel is glass shards and spikes so there is no climbing over. I think we just have to wait it out a bit. Eventually we'll be given leave to visit the city and have free time. Then we can run away but... We have to wait."

"No," I said shaking my head. My eyes wanted to water but I wouldn't let them. "No," I said again turning to face the wall. I was never going to make it that long. I was going to die here. My parents would never know what happened to me. I must have fallen asleep eventually but I still remember staring at that wall all night and try not to think *anything*.

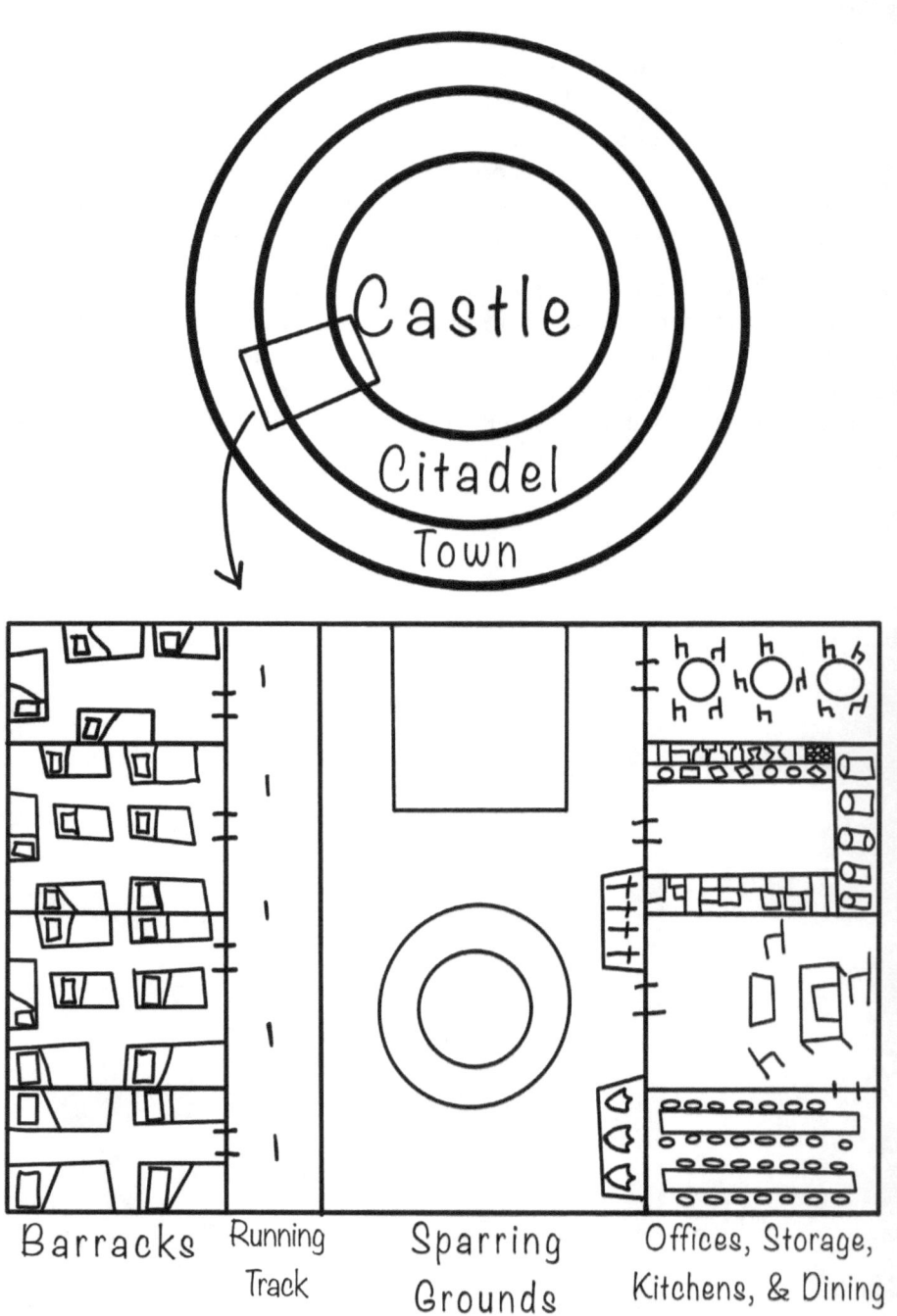

Castle

Citadel

Town

Barracks Running Track Sparring Grounds Offices, Storage, Kitchens, & Dining

2

I was pulled from sparing the next day and I didn't know what to think. They didn't kick people out so there wasn't that hope. Maybe I was going to receive a specialized punishment. Maybe they'd just kill me. But when I got to my trainer's office only Jol was there and the look on his face was the softest sneer I'd ever seen. He felt bad for me.

"Sit down," he said and after being screamed at for a couple days it felt like a damn whisper. I sat down. If I'd learned anything, it was to do a thing as soon as I was told to do it. "How is it going?" he asked rhetorically, I was sure, but I answered anyway.

"Poorly, Mage."

"What's going wrong?"

"I'm too slow, too stupid, and too ugly, Sir," I added the 'Sir' without thinking. I'd just repeated that same sentence so many times that the 'Sir' got added on. His eyebrows furrowed. It was such a welcome, familiar sight that I thought about smiling. I didn't. I don't know that I could have at that moment.

Jol looked at me then. He really looked at me and I wonder what he thought. Maybe he felt some weird responsibility. He was the one who had signed me up and left me. Maybe it was pity. Either way he left the room without a word but not before he patted my shoulder. I *almost* didn't flinch. I don't know what Jol said or who he said it to but things were different after that. I realized later how much pull Jol actually had to accomplish what he did.

That afternoon I didn't return to class with the warrior children, instead I was called to my trainer's office again. This time there as only my trainer and a tall man I'd never met. He had brown hair tied back at his neck. His beard was neat and trim. All of him was neat and trim. He was different than anyone else I'd met in Morland.

"This is Hezekiah," my trainer said unable to wipe all the shock from his own face. I nodded my head at him once and then lowered my gaze. I had no idea who the man was but if my trainer was nervous, I should be petrified.

"I will be taking over your training. Come with me," Hezekiah said. I followed him, unsure what fresh hell awaited me but I was taken out of the Citadel and to a pub.

"What will it be?" the bar maid asked as she walked over. She stopped short when she saw Hezekiah but quickly recovered. "Our special today is beef stew with root vegetables. I'm so sorry but we are out of the honeyed bread. We only have plain. But I'm sure I could get the cook to make you another loaf. We didn't know you'd be coming today or we would, of course, have saved our best for..."

"The plain is fine," Hezekiah said raising his hand to save the women from more apologizing. "We'll have two stews. The kid will have a watered ale and I'll have the house wine." The food came quickly and Hezekiah placed a stew, the watered ale, and half the loaf in front of me.

"You are the Mage's boy?" he asked looking me over as I cautiously ate the food. I hated throwing up and I did most days after the workout but it seemed rude not to eat it and it was ten times better than what they'd been feeding us.

I wasn't sure what to say to that. So I told the truth. "He found me."

"Do you know who I am?" he asked.

I shook my head. That seemed to surprise him. I hoped I wouldn't be punished for that.

"I'm the General's son."

My mouth dropped open. The General's son. I know that that doesn't mean anything to you but Morland has one General and he has one son.

I knew enough about my new world to know who he was now. Hezekiah, the General's son was the best swordsman in the whole country. Better than his father, the General. Better than every instructor who'd beat me so effortlessly. His skill was so far beyond my understanding it was like an ant trying to understand how hot the sun really was.

"But," he continued at my silence, "even I am not immune to a favor from the Mage. I'll be training you from here on out. Or until you are capable enough to join your class and stop being a disgrace to the Mage. Do you understand?"

I nodded.

"Good. We start tomorrow," he nodded his head to the untouched ale and I now drank it readily. A whole afternoon off. I wondered if it was Christmas.

Hezekiah

Instead of yelling at me and then beating me, Hezekiah did a lot of talking. He broke it down to small pieces until it clicked. He started with the running.

"You need endurance. There is no way to get around it. If you keep getting winded in training then you'll never be able to master any of the skills. First thing we do is change your diet. That gruel from the Citadel kitchen wouldn't keep a dog alive. Fruits, Vegetable, Meat. Once your body is being fueled you'll be surprised how your energy increases. And simply running is not going to do it. It's lazy and I wish the trainers would take more time. You need to strengthen your whole body. Being able to run a mile quickly does not mean you'll have the strength to wield a sword at the end of it."

My days drastically changed. Hezekiah never yelled. That was the biggest part and he spoke to me like a man and I finally started to feel like one or a human again, at least. I moved into his quarters in the Citadel and slept on a mat near the fire.

We had breakfast together then ran two laps around the Citadel to warm up. Then we'd do strength training exercises. At first he gave me as many water breaks as I wanted and amazingly after a week I stopped needing to make the excuse.

After that we started running in the country. It was so much easier than circling the Citadel over and over. Seeing trees and feeling the wind was... it was a gift. He'd talk to me about life while we ran. I was always too winded to speak but I listened. He ran like he was strolling in the park.

"I know this life is hard," he said one day. "My father dropped me off when I was five." I wondered why he was telling me all this. Maybe it was part of his deal with the Mage, small talk. "I knew even then that the only way I'd see my father again was if I became a great warrior. So I trained harder than the boys that were five years older than me. That's how you become the best, Derek. You need to find a reason. Why are you doing this?"

I opened my mouth and closed it. I had no idea why I was doing it. I'd thought I was only doing it because there was no backing out. I was signed up and there was no escape clause. If I'd been pressed for a reason the previous week, I would have said that I just didn't want to die. But now...

"I want to be your equal. And I want to be my own master." The words came out unbidden. Was that what I really wanted? The first part for sure. Hezekiah was the coolest man I'd ever met. He was my hero. I wanted to be exactly like him. And the second part? It was also true. I wanted to be strong enough so no one could ever boss me around again. When I was my own master I could use my time to search for the tree home.

"Hmm," he said giving me an appraising look. "Those are admirable goals. I look forward to the day. But no man is really his own master. Even my father bows to the Queen. But there is a certain amount of freedom you'll gain. And it will feel like being your own master."

Within a month I was with the guys my own age but Hezekiah didn't abandon me. I'd expected him to. I was now at the top of my class and after I was fourteen (in another month) I'd be given a rank and assignments and freedom to explore the city. I'd given up on the idea of running away. If I was stuck in Morland, it was better to be fed with a roof over my head than a poor beggar boy like I'd seen on the streets.

And I would get two free days a month and I could use those to look for the way home. Free days! The idea was mind-blowing. It seemed like the life of kings. But Hezekiah took my free days and we trained together and I didn't mind. It became more sparing and sword lore than running and I was so grateful for his time. After another month, the Mage came.

My body was toned and my face was almost unrecognizable even to myself. I looked like a man. Jol's eyes flicked around the training area and landed on me after he'd passed me twice. He walked over and nodded his head.

"How is it going?"

"Very well, Mage," I said.

"Let's see," Jol removed his cape and freed the sword at his side. I was ready with my own blade in an instant. One of Hezekiah's favorite ways to train was to attack when I didn't expect it. Jol was going to have to be a lot quicker than that to best me, I'd thought. But as usual I was wrong. I realized how much Hezekiah had been holding back when after four seconds, Jol had me knocked on my back. I stood up and we tried again. I was more ready this time and we lasted for two minutes. Sweat was coming down my face and all it took was one misstep. He flicked my sword away and I felt steel at my neck.

"I yield," I said instantly.

Hezekiah walked out smiling and picked up my sword. The Mage raised his eyebrows and then nodded. *Everyone* stopped what they were doing to watch. They could have sold tickets for a sparring match between Jol and Hezekiah. If Jol had struck like a tornado, then Hezekiah was a nuke. I didn't just hear their swords clashing, I felt it. Hezekiah was a machine and he'd been taking me through the babiest baby steps. I had so much left to learn.

Jol yielded after five minutes and the two men talked quietly to the side and then shook hands. Hezekiah nodded his head at me and then was gone. I wouldn't see him again for a long time. His task was completed and I was returned full time to the herd. It was hard at first to submit to the harsh ways of the Citadel. But I was the top of the class and even if it made me a target it also meant I wasn't vomiting every day. It's the little things in life.

Garrison

1

I was fourteen and a half when I met Garrison. I was crushing it at the Citadel or more accurately they were trying to kill me less. It hadn't been easy to adjust after Hezekiah left. It was hard to bow my will to small-minded idiots when I'd met a real man, a teacher I could respect. I now saw my instructors at the Citadel for what they were, imposters and cowards. I found I no longer cared what they thought of me. Now when they whipped me it wasn't for being the worst. It was because they couldn't break me. But they liked to try.

Garrison and I each tell this story differently but I wasn't the one running for my life so I feel like I remember it more clearly than he does. Garrison is a thug. He's a dark haired, wily, slippery idiot. He was also my best friend for a long time. He's also a thief. Jol was actually looking for *him* the day he found me in the woods. But Jol doesn't know that.

It was one of my rare free days and I usually used them to run the forest, looking for my damn tree. But this day I was in town just minding my own business when this dark haired streak comes around the corner followed by several soldiers. In the moment before we crashed into each other I saw him, really saw him. He was scared. He was thin. And there was a deep hunger in his eyes.

"There you are. It's about time," I said detangling from the impact of our collision. I did not know this kid and I was shocked at the words coming out of my mouth. He just stared at me, also bewildered by my actions. The soldiers were moving towards us, catching their breaths as they walked over.

"Jol has been waiting a week for you to arrive. Where have you been? It's not a good idea to keep your uncle waiting. Come on," I said ignoring the soldiers and jerking my attacker before me by his shirt's collar. I didn't know the two men but I'm sure they knew me. Not many men use Jol's name. I held on to the kid's shirt and walked purposely away. I imagined the guards looking between themselves and then shrugging. I didn't look back to check.

I'd used the magic word. I tried not to do it often. I worried Jol would remove his protection. But it had worked. It was well known that Jol had signed me into the Citadel and that he visited from time to time. I'd probably just saved the kid's life. He tried to shake out of my grip once we were around the corner but I didn't let him. I... I don't know why.

I took a good look at him and saw that he was skin and bones. He didn't even have shoes and it was winter. My luck suddenly didn't seem so bad. Maybe if Jol hadn't been there in the woods that day looking for Garrison than I would have died, lost and cold in those woods.

2

Garrison thought I was going to murder him or something. I didn't know that until later. I'd imagined that he saw me as his patron saint. Here I was getting him stew and ale and buying him cheap boots. But he thought I was some crazy aristocrat who was going to sell him to the meat shop once I'd fattened him up. It shows how far I'd come in my time at the Citadel that I was mistaken as a wealthy man instead of a beaten scrawny kid.

Garrison is actually four months older than me. He tried to lord it over me but when he joined the Citadel and struggled as I had, he was glad for private lessons from me. It felt like I was one step closer to being Hezekiah. I tried to remember everything he'd taught me so I could ease Garrison's way. Garrison tells me that I was a garbage teacher and maybe I was but Garrison was a quick study and soon we were sparing together in earnest. He made me the swordsman I became. We each had this fire in us to be better. To be stronger. To protect ourselves from what the world had done to us so far.

Garrison was an orphan or so he assumed. He'd been alone as long as he could remember, stealing to survive. He didn't stop stealing just because he had three meals a day and pay from the Citadel. I found it hilariously hypocritical. When we were fifteen we were tasked with patrolling the streets, catching thieves, calming fights, keeping the peace. But when we weren't on duty we did all of those things, stole, fought, and caused havoc. I didn't mind. I didn't know it but before Garrison I'd been bored out of my mind.

My soul *really* disliked him at first. And he didn't really dislike anyone. I wondered if he could be jealous that I didn't need him as much. I don't know if he can feel jealousy but if he can dislike someone, then he can probably be jealous too. Eventually he came around. I'm sure it was hard because Garrison couldn't see my soul. No one but me could see or hear him and I didn't tell Garrison about my soul or my home. So I was talking less to my soul and maybe he was lonely.

What Derek saw

pat
pat

Oh, mighty sir! I am not worthy of such kindness. Ever will I serve thee!

What Garrison saw

1. Too clean
(Rich and corrupt)
2. Too quick with lies
(Hiding something)
3. Too generous
(Ulterior motive)
Only option:
kill him before he eats me.

It wasn't that I didn't trust Garrison. I mean I didn't trust him. He'd probably sell me out to the highest bidder if he found out I was from another planet. But it wasn't just that. I started to get this anxiety in the pit of my stomach that someone from Morland was going to find the way back to Earth and ruin it. It made my forest excursions more frantic and it felt like a race. What if all the horrible wrongness of Morland crept into Earth? I didn't know if I was ever going to go home but I sure as hell didn't want anything bad to happen to it. I loved Earth. I didn't ever think about it, of course. But I worried about it, without naming it.

3

The best example I can think of about the nature of Garrison and I's relationship is Julie. We were competitive in everything and I mean everything: Food, Drink, Patrol, Swordsmanship, Women. Julie was the new apprentice at the bakery close to our favorite pub, the Starlight. It's a dumb name but they let you drink as much as you want and fight until you can't stand. Sometimes when you are a teenager trapped in an army you can't leave, on a planet you can't escape, you just have to drink a lot and punch your best friend in the face every once in a while.

We both noticed immediately when Julie arrived. One of Hezekiah's biggest lessons was observance. It was mostly for fighting application but it had a way of leaking over into everything. If I am clever, then Garrison is sly. I didn't stand a chance in a charm-off.

First off, I'm a redhead so there is a certain amount of snarkiness and sass in my genetic makeup. I've also got the textbook short temper. I'm very sarcastic and quick with a come-back. Also I'm soulless or soul-adjacent and that leaves a hollowness that I think people can sense.

Garrison can literally ooze charm when he wants to. He can make anyone like him. It helps that he filled out into the tall, dark, and handsome archetype.

We each acted like fools to try and woo her and for her part she liked the attention of two suitors but I think she knew we were both messing around. We weren't playing for keeps, only fun, and she was a smart enough girl to know that we would only spell trouble for her. She stayed in a small room above the bakery and her mistress, Mrs. Ludmen, was not amused with us.

When her husband was out of town, she frequented the Starlight so where Julie only *thought* we might be trouble, Mrs. Ludmen *knew* we were trouble. After we started courting Julie, Mrs. Ludmen bought some new members to the household. She wanted to protect her young apprentice. Garrison and I were not aware of this fact but we thought we were, oh so, observant. Idiots.

My soul had started to wander off on his own more often when Garrison and I became close and he was gone that night. We started the evening at the Starlight and after a couple hours of drinking Garrison had an epiphany. He grabbed my face and jumped up still holding it.

"I figured it out!" he said.

"Figured wha ow?" I said through my squished face.

"How to win Julie!" he yelled running off but not before he released my face. I fell over and stumbled after him. We'd been at the Starlight *a long time* already at this point. I was confused when he started off running in the opposite direction of the bakery but he didn't go far.

The Queen and Country Inn was on the other side of the road. We weren't allowed to go in there unless we were sober and in our uniforms. But he didn't go inside. He took out the dagger he kept in his boot and started sawing at the flower bush out front. I just stared at him from the Starlight's stoop.

"What in the name of..." I said just watching him mutilate the plants but then my intoxicated brain caught up with his and I was over there cutting my own bouquet. I didn't really want Julie. There were plenty of girls I could have that thought Garrison was a git and that made it easier. But I couldn't let him win. Garrison had everything, it seemed to me in that moment. He was my equal in swordsmanship and hand-to-hand fighting. He was likable and nice. He had his soul. It was just one thing too many.

So I punched him in the face and ran for the bakery with four broken roses in my hand. It took him a good minute to right himself and by then I was scaling the back wall of the shop and climbing towards her room. My mind had cleared and it seemed like if I could have Julie then I won. It wasn't just beating Garrison. It was beating Morland. Since my soul separated from me, my mind had drawn a connection to lust and hate. I hated Morland and everything in it. So I hated Julie but I also wanted her.

Garrison caught up and we both stumbled into the window together. We were really loud and it didn't help that we were cursing at each other. Julie let out a squeal and lit her lantern. I had Garrison in a headlock and he was biting the inside of my elbow hard enough to make me bleed. We both straightened and threw the flowers at her feet.

This was it. She was going to pick one of us to stay. We'd won her over with our bravery and daring. We'd brought her flowers and broken the rules. Girls loved that kind of thing. We held our breaths and... she screamed. What we hadn't noticed in our brawling entry into the room were the two large hounds at the foot of her bed and unbeknownst to us the two additional large hounds in the kitchen downstairs.

The dogs took their signal and lunged for us. Garrison kicked me towards them and dove out of the window. The first dog's mouth was open in a bark and Garrison's kick sent me right towards her. She bit down hard on my collarbone and I screamed. Her sister was biting my bicep and I pulled out my dagger and sloppily gutted them both before rolling out the window.

By then the whole household was awake and running up the stairs. I had a minute head start before the dogs would be released into the streets. I was bleeding like a bloody fountain and I would be easy to find.

It was all over. I'd be thrown in prison and then I'd been beaten by my once friends who were guarding me. I'd have nothing and no one. The Mage wouldn't save me. What skills did I have but killing things? And no one was allowed to kill things except the Queen's men. I'd thought that I had nothing in Morland but that was until I'd thrown it all away to beat my friend.

Some friend. If he hadn't have kicked me, I would have gotten out of the window in time. No one but Julie had seen us and if we weren't caught red-handed then all she'd have was a tale of two men in her bedroom at night. And she wasn't a fool. But now I was going to get caught. Hell, I might even die. Medicine in Morland was crap and I was bleeding a lot.

I didn't know which way I should run. I started towards the Citadel but they wouldn't let me in or worse they would and I'd be closer to judgement when the time came. I was going to die. Tears starting falling from my eyes and I'm sure it was from the pain.

At the crossroads before the Citadel, a hand grabbed my bad arm and pulled me into the alleyway. I bit back a yell at the pain and saw

Garrison. I lifted my dagger with a shaky hand. It was still covered in hound blood and I hadn't noticed I was still clutching it. He had probably been waiting a long time to finish me off. And here was his chance. But I was sure as hell going to try to take him with me.

"I'm not going to kill you, you bleeding idiot!" he said easily disarming me. "I'm trying to save your stupid life." He tried to pull me along but now that I'd stopped running my feet wouldn't start back up again.

"Great," he said sarcastically coming around my good side to support me. "You weigh a million pounds when you pass out. Stay awake." He took off his jacket and slipped it on me and raised the hood. Then he led me deeper and deeper through the small back alleys that good people didn't know so well as us. Then he knocked three times at a door I knew very well.

"Well," said a busty brunette with raised eyebrows, Bella was Garrison's favorite. Jillian was mine. But she wasn't there to see me bleeding a river in their back room. "It's a little late isn't it, solider?" she said pulling us in.

"We need a room, Bella," Garrison said lifting my hood.

She cursed once and lifted my bad arm to help me upstairs. I thought I might die as we climbed. Mrs. Black, named after her black heart, came into the room to get the matter of payment sorted when she saw the situation and cursed a storm herself. She wasn't really black hearted, well maybe every madam is a bit but she saved my life. She called the only doctor that would take care of her girls and then I passed out.

I wish I could include a picture diagraming all of my scars, but they are all gone now, of course. (Spoiler. I'll let you chew on that in your mind.) So I'll tell you about them. The one on my neck and shoulder from the first dog is ugly and ragged. That's what you get from a doctor who hides in the shadows and saves your life for free. My back is a network of lighter scars from my slow feet and stubborn will.

The scar on my bicep looks like a drunk child's attempt at connect the dots. The one of my side is the most important and the one I miss most. And there are others but you get the picture. Thankfully none of them marred my handsome face, not like one that Garrison will get... Every coin has two sides, doesn't it?

rt

The Map of Scars

Front   Back

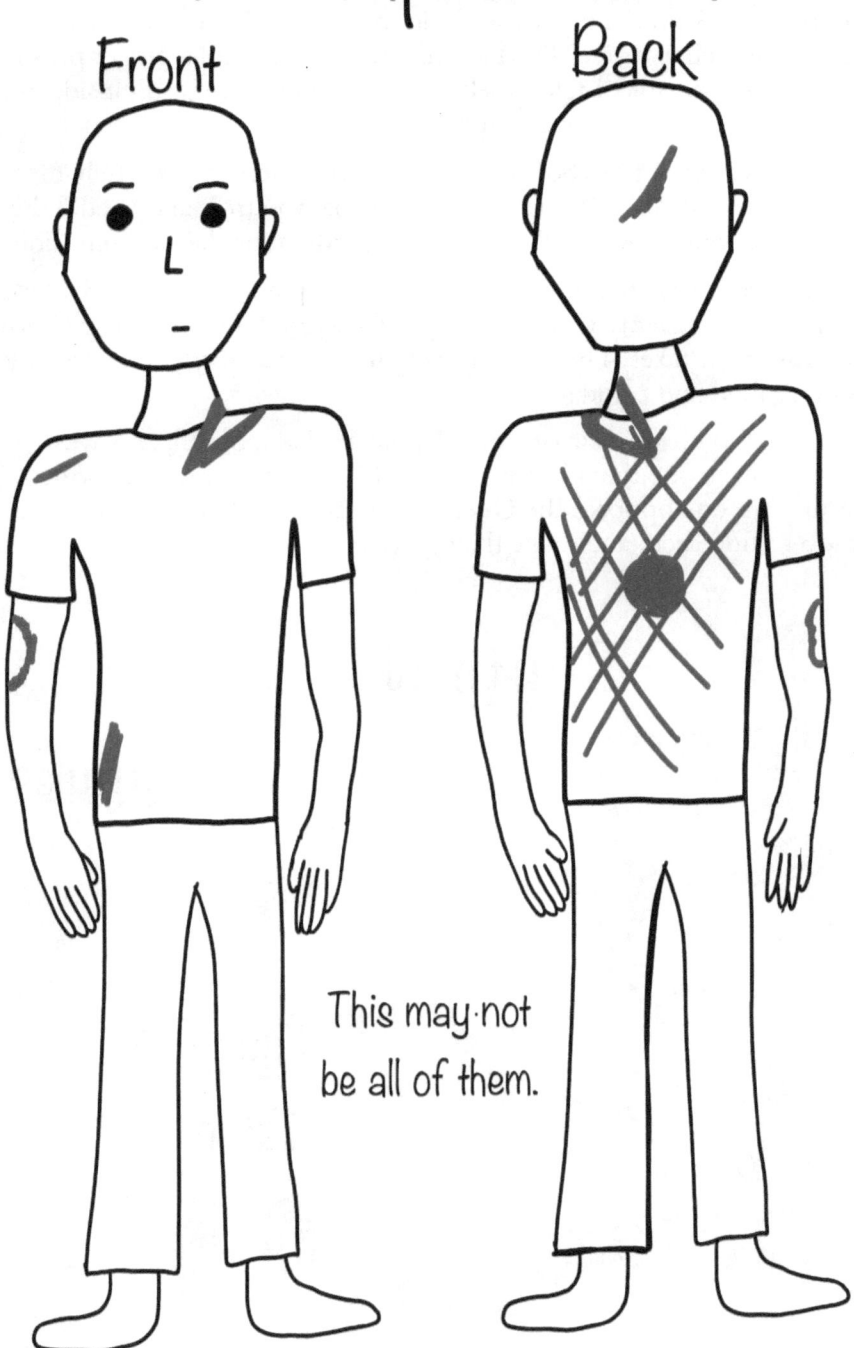

This may not
be all of them.

4

Garrison's scar was my fault. It was my fault in a different way than my scars from the night with Julie were his fault. He didn't blame me for it. Which is worse. The fact that he's scarred and a bigger person than me is unbearable. I tell myself it's because his soul is still inside but I don't think I was that good before.

Anyway back to it. So we were seventeen and had been fully men for a year at least. We'd been moved off of baby patrols and we did the Queen's real work now, quelling the ever resurgent pockets of rebellion.

It amazed me that it kept happening. People were so stupid. She'd been ruling for seventy years and they still tried to hide their magic born and refuse their taxes. The nomads were the worst. Mostly because they moved around and could avoid her.

There are four sects of nomads: North, East, South, and West. They only have one thing in common. They are even more stubborn than me. No one opposes the Queen as blatantly as they do. And it was our job to find them and make them pay

South Nomads

Location

South Coast

Out to sea

Southern Islands

Attributes

Dark skin

South accent (Scottish)

Sailors

Difficulty to catch

Easy

South Nomads

The South nomads are the easiest to catch because they never moved. They inhabit the whole South Coast. Because they don't move their insurrection is slower and more calculating. So it's harder to catch them *at it*. Whenever we got close they were faster and were already out to sea.

They are the best seamen in all of Morland. Their trade keeps the country supplied with all its needs which is why they aren't all dead. They transport coal from the north and bring fish and vegetables from the south. They are Morland's delivery service and trading hub.

They are dark skinned from generations at sea and their Scottish accents are just another strange link to Earth and Morland. Why are there different English dialects here? Why do they speak English at all? Why is everyone human? How does Earth have a portal leading to Morland? How many people before me have travelled my path? Everyone here? Is every soul on Morland a descendent of portal traveller like myself? No one has any answers, of course, not that I ask.

The South nomads are my favorite. They somehow managed to keep their culture and sense of identity even with all the Queen has done to quell them. That's why she hates them so much. That's why they are a threat to her.

I said that the South nomads keep Morland supplied because of trading but it's not really trading because there is no one else here. Morland is the name of the planet *and* the country. Every inch of the land on this planet is called Morland. There isn't another country on the opposite side of the world planning to come and free us. It's all just us. The South nomads sail from the south islands up the east or west coast to the north mountain and bring the specialties of each region to the capitol.

As a solider of the Queen, my job was to shake them up, remind them who was in charge, take taxes, and show everyone watching that the South nomads were nothing special and there were consequences for helping them.

North Nomads

Location

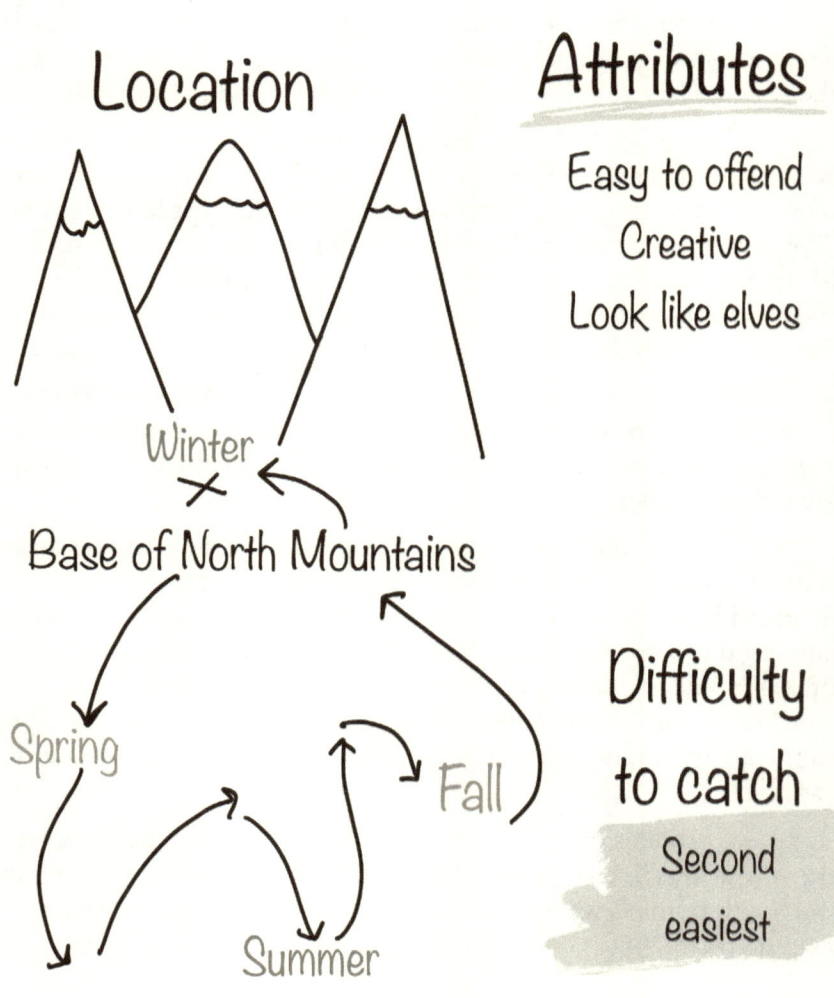

Winter

✗

Base of North Mountains

Spring

Summer

Fall

Attributes

Easy to offend
Creative
Look like elves

Difficulty to catch

Second easiest

North Nomads

The North nomads are the second easiest to catch. They travel the land during the warm months but they always camp in the mountains in the winter. Finding a glen of them all bunked down in their assumed safety could get you a promotion.

The first time we came across a glen of them, I'd thought for a dumb second that they were elves. Every one of them had pale skin and dark hair and just an air about them. They seemed different than me. They weren't elves, of course. They were just humans, still bled red.

The Queen hates the North nomads less than the South but she still sees red when they don't pay their taxes and when their creative products cause problems. They paint, sing, and play music about any topic they want, including the Queen. She doesn't want them dead, well she does but she doesn't order her men to kill them. She wants them imprisoned or obedient.

So we rough them up and see which path they are going to take. Their pride is so strong that most times they are too offended to bow to the queen. But the time we found a glen of Northies they thankfully caved after a short fight. The idea of transporting all the men, women, and children to the prison was an upsetting idea. Nomads as a whole do poorly surrounded by stone walls. It's like they need another element to survive beyond the air, water, and food that the rest of us need. They need fresh air and sunshine and freedom.

East Nomads

Location

Anywhere.

Everywhere

Attributes

Kind

Travel

Healers

Pink hair on women

Difficulty
to catch

Almost

hardest

East Nomads

The East nomads are *almost* the hardest to catch. They never stop moving. Ever. One city to the next to the next to the next. It's like they are following a trail made out of wind. The thing that always trips them up is their kindness. (You can't see me shaking my head but I am.)

They are the best healers in the land. Not magic healers but just good doctors. It's usually the *exact* people they had *just* treated who send us a note that they've been there. People are bastards. And yet the Easties don't stop helping people. It's like they can't help it. Where I'm from in Waxhaw, North Carolina we'd say "Bless their hearts."

The East nomads have the most distinctive look, white-blond hair on the men and cotton-candy-pink hair for the women. Yeah, pink hair. They dye it, I'm sure. But it's the worst way to look if you are openly flouting the monarch.

People are stupid, especially these ones. They don't pay their taxes and they trickle hope behind them. Healing people's physical pains feels so 'almost' magical that is wakens hope in the people. The East nomads Irish accents probably help, though it's not called that of course. It's just called an East accent. There must be another portal from Earth to Morland somewhere in the United Kingdom. I mean how else are there three different English dialects? Morland doesn't make any sense.

West Nomads

Attributes

Tan
Reclusive
Secrets?

Location

W

West
Plains

Difficulty
to catch

Hardest

West Nomads

The West nomads are the hardest to catch *because* they never move and there are so few of them. They live in the West Plains and in all my traveling of Morland I've not even ventured a league into it. It's a barren, desert land. When magic ebbed from the planet seventy years ago something happened to the West Plains. I think there must have been some enchanted water source or something. Now in its current state it is unlivable. Well obviously it's not because there are still bands of Westies that live there. But I have no idea how.

They are tan skinned and reclusive. I've seen maybe a handful of them, ever. The Queen has almost given up on them. Her soldiers can't go far into the Plains and honestly the West nomads cause no trouble so I say let them be. Although no one cares what I say and I don't speak dissension out loud. It's probably a miracle but I've learned at least this lesson from others instead of doing each mistake myself: Don't mess with the Queen.

5

But back to Garrison, right? Can you tell that I have trouble talking about my faults and my feelings? Emotional repression, the doctors will name it later. Whatever. So we were hunting nomads and this was a hunt that felt less gross than the others. A band of West nomads had crossed the Plains and were killing and robbing villages. It was strange, not the kind of thing I'd ever heard them do before. So our troop was sent to investigate.

I was the leader of our six-man group. Garrison hated this. He hated this so much it would keep him up at night. I know this because we all shared a bunkhouse at the Citadel and Garrison grinds his teeth when he's upset. It makes me smile even now to remember it. I'm a monster.

I'd beaten Garrison for command of our small troop easily. It was easy because Garrison had been *happy*. Happy people are sloppy and lazy. Whereas I was a miserable, bitter jerk whose only hobbies were training, drinking alcohol, and looking for my tree. I'd lost my taste for women after the hound incident.

I trained harder and longer than Garrison on our training days and I worked out and ran the woods during our free days. Garrison went to shows and dinner with other soldiers. He read books and listened to musicians. He took his time wooing women. He didn't stand a chance against me.

We had to spar against each other as the last two options for lead rank. It was only a spar and not even to first blood. It was just a display of ability. But when Garrison got close I broke his nose with my elbow and made him submit as I pinned him face down. He was mad for a long while after that. But I told myself he couldn't have wanted it as much as I did. Otherwise he would have broken my nose first.

6

"This is a weird lead. Westies killing people..." Garrison said that night as we ate our rations without a fire. We were close and we all knew that the cold was better than an ambush.

Everyone nodded at Garrison's comment. I hated when he did that. It felt like he was trying to make a coup attempt. If I'm the harsh leader, he's the understanding second who is always there to listen. But he was still my best friend and I nod. But I didn't let his comment sit.

"There must be more we don't know. Whatever we find I'll match it against other reports that have come in recently. Maybe Hezekiah has heard of something."

That's right, remember who I am. They may all think Garrison is still Jol's nephew but I'm his ward *and* Hezekiah's apprentice, so I win. Garrison's eyes flicked to mine and I saw his thoughts as he saw mine. *This isn't the end.*

"I just think we need to be careful tomorrow, is all," he said. "Something is off about this. When have we ever heard of a Westie leaving the Plains for anything, let alone a pillaging spree? Doesn't it set of your intuition? Doesn't it raise your hackles at all? I just think that we don't have all the information. I'm not saying they kept it from us but I think there is more to it."

"We'll do as we are told," I told Garrison. "We are here for a mission and we'll accomplish it. I don't care if you are afraid but Westies aren't boogeymen, they are just flesh and blood men." All five sets of eyes rest on me a moment and I realize that 'boogeyman' must have been a misstep. I so rarely say an 'Earth' thing but how can I know everything that is different when so much is the same.

"What's a boogeyman?" Len said. He was not trying to undermine me. He's just an idiot and doesn't want to be left out anything. Len is a year younger than us but he doesn't look it. He's big and strong and not much more than that.

"It's like a nightmare for children. Did some old woman not threaten you to go to bed or the boogeymen would come for you?" As soon as the words are out of my mouth, I know this is a worse mistake. A critical mistake. None of these men had women to fuss over them, to care what time they went to bed. It's a more alien comment than the boogeyman and it's just divided us.

They don't know my past. All they know is my unexplainable tie to the Mage. But to tell them that I had a mother who cared about me is like saying I cut my teeth on diamonds and was rocked on a golden rocking horse.

I don't say anything else and they don't ask. But I hate that I just gave Garrison a victory. I knew he was just storing this away for later. I could almost hear it. "How can Derek understand us? He didn't have the upbringing we had. He must be some spoiled brat left by his parents. He doesn't know what we've lived through." And the truth is that I don't. I don't think about my childhood but god knows it was better than Garrison's street urchin existence before he met me. I soften towards him for a moment. Maybe he doesn't have everything I want.

My soul reamed me out as we got ready for bed. It felt like his official job title: Scolder Extraordinaire.

"What was that about?" he said with raised eyebrows. He knew what it was about but he was trying this psychology technique where he tried to get me to answer questions about why I was doing things in an attempt that I would understand how stupid my reasons were. It rarely worked.

I turned to my side so my voice wouldn't carry to the others. "He's doing it again," I said. "Planting doubt."

"You sound like a child. Do you realize that?" he said without a smile. He was the only one allowed to speak to me that way and that was because I couldn't actual make him stop. "You sound like a crazy, paranoid child. Garrison only said one thing and he was right. And you know it! Why do you play these juvenile mind games with him? What would Hezekiah do in this situation? What would he do with a number two like Garrison, who may or not may be plotting against him?"

I pounded my fist into the ground and bit my tongue. He knew I couldn't yell at him without losing further face. "What do you know, soul? You don't understand what it's like for me?" I hissed at him.

"Who but me can understand you, you stupid idiot?" he said smiling now. He thought 'stupid idiot' was a term of endearment or something. Like a cute nickname. I did not.

"You have no troubles. No concerns," I whispered loudly. "You just float through life doing whatever you please wherever you want. You don't have a job. You don't have to train. All you do is yell at me. That's your only job. You can't possibly understand what it's like to live in Morland. You don't know the pressure I feel. You are just a soul. You don't know how stressful living is! You are a ghost! Who are you to tell me what to do?"

The hurt registered wide open on his face, my face. No one else on Morland had ever seen my face look so vulnerable and hurt. He was sensitive about that, the fact that he was just a ghost. The fact that he had no purpose and no friends but me and nothing to do but watch. And I'd just thrown that in his face.

He pulled his mask down after a moment. It wasn't as good as mine but it was enough to make me feel bad. I could still be made to feel bad it just took a lot to do it. And hurting my soul was one way.

I started to search for an apology in my black soulless depths but he was gone. He was able to say whatever he wanted to me but he was also able to leave whenever he wanted. I felt a wave of lostness come over me, the child-like fear of losing my mom in the grocery store. I wished that I wasn't so stubborn and so cruel and so callous. But I am what I am, right?

The next day we were all a little anxious despite the sunshine. They don't know that I am. My feelings are hidden behind so many layers of walls, I sometimes forget what I'm feeling. But Garrison is anxious; I can tell by how he's locked his jaw. He looks mean when he's anxious. He looks a little like me, I think, like a brother I didn't know I had. That's how I think of him. As much as we compete with each other, I care about him. As much as I can care about anyone that is.

Not enough.

I notice the trap at the same time Garrison does, we share a look and all our issues are tabled for the moment. We got off our horses and examined it. The string was tied close to the ground and led up the tree to an Indiana-Jones-style spike device.

"What the hell?" Cort says touching the fiber gently. His dark skin makes the light fiber pop as he studies it closely. He's from the South Coast originally, probably not a South nomad but who in my troop knows his own father? I lean closer for his opinion. He knows an unimaginable amount more about Morland than I do. "This is some high quality string. You wouldn't have even seen it if the sun wasn't shining. I've never seen anything like this. How the hell do Westies get near-invisible string?"

"But more importantly we were supposed to beat them here," Andrew said touching a muddy footprint on the ground and then rubbing his face with the same hand leaving a trail of mud across his face. Andrew was always dirty. I've never seen him bathe. His hair was probably blond but it was so caked with... I don't know, debris? that it was always a dark muddy brown. He looked around and started biting his nails. Fin growls and almost shakes. Andrew bites his nails all the time and it drives Fin absolutely crazy.

Fin takes immaculate care of himself. If Garrison and I think we are good looking, Fin is a model. Besides himself, he doesn't really care about anything. We have that in common. So when he speaks next I'm tempted to listen. "This isn't right, like Garrison said. Something's not right." And then he cited Garrison and I didn't want to listen anymore.

If he'd just said "This isn't right. Something's not right." I would have agreed and he'd still be alive. He didn't know this and neither did I. But I'm just so stubborn, remember, and his comments made me sink in my heels. We weren't leaving because 'Garrison said'.

I heard Garrison exhale a groan and it made me smile. He knew me so well.

"I'm sorry that you miss the comforts of your beauty regime, Fin but we are not here on holiday. We have a mission and a task and we will complete it. Things don't make sense because we have only just started. You don't stop a puzzle because the pieces aren't matched up yet. You have eyes, don't you, Fin?" He flinched. He doesn't know what he's done to gain my rage but he doesn't move. None of them do. This isn't the first time.

"And you have a brain, don't you, Fin? So use it. Bloody hell. I didn't know my troop was a bunch of frightened children who didn't know their head from their ass. Move out," I said leading my horse by the reigns around the booby trapped tree.

No one spoke much for the rest of the trip. Not when we saw another thirty traps and not when we saw at least a dozen sets of hoof prints. I think they were hoping I'd relent, that I'd cave. Garrison and I were playing a game of chicken but he wasn't sure if I'd swerve or not. He didn't know if I'd knowingly plow us all to our deaths so he spoke first. I cursed him for it in my head. Five more minutes, I'd said to myself. I was only making us walk until midday. You couldn't have waited five bloody minutes, Garrison?

"Derek..." Garrison said trying to hide the rage behind his eyes. I didn't get a chance to answer because the arrows started flying. My troop was well trained but an arrow ambush is a hard thing to parry. Fin took one to the heart and fell back without a twitch. Andrew, Len, and Garrison dove to the right, while Cort and I dove to the left.

There were at least twenty of them. We were going to die and they weren't even bloody nomads. We'd been sent to kill our own. They were soldiers, about five to ten years older than us. We wouldn't have stood a chance if not for my soul. He came back and I heard his voice like a clear bell amidst the clash and cry of battle.

"Derek. Four things," he said walking towards me as he unconsciously dodged the action. He could not touch or be touched by them but it was probably hard to walk face first into a sword swing. I turned my back to him to pull my sword free from the spine of a solider. I didn't need to see my soul I just needed to hear what he'd found out.

"One. There are twelve barrels of oil under that pile of leaves to your right. There isn't a match nearby so you'll have to light it with flint.

Two. Their leader is the man with the red band on his sleeve. If he dies they will be severely demoralized. It will help.

Three. There are several of those spike contraptions still unactivated. Tell Cort to shoot them all down.

Four. I told you so."

Asshole. But he'd just saved us. Thankfully Cort was next to me so I told him as quietly as I could about the untriggered traps. He nodded and I covered him so he could loose his bow. During the activity of the spike booby traps falling on their men I was able to break through to the red-sleeved leader.

He'd been keeping to the back firing arrows and he wasn't pleased to have a visitor. I'm sure I looked an absolute terror walking toward him with two bloody swords swinging in my hands. He tried to back away but he was an archer not a swordsman. I shattered his bow as he held it as a shield and I shoved both swords to slice off his head.

Nothing breaks a man like seeing his leader's head removed from his body. I didn't even feel bad. These men had turned their back on their country. They'd started to hurt and rob the people they were supposed to be protecting. It wasn't like they were gathering rebels with fliers and rallies. They were killing families and taking their livestock and possessions. They deserved to be flayed like pigs.

"He'd dead!" I yelled kicking his head away. To his men's credit they didn't stop completely but their hesitation and shock was enough, especially with the finale. I caught Garrison's eye. I couldn't tell him about the coming explosion from how far away he was but I used our code for retreat, a quick head jerk to the left. I told Cort to shoot one more arrow, this one on fire. I didn't see Andrew or Len but they'd been with Garrison and Garrison looked after his people. I shouldn't have been so hard on him. I kept seeing Fin fall flat like a pancake on repeat over and over everywhere I looked.

Cort's shot was true and the explosion was louder than it was damaging but by the time the smoke cleared we were running back to our horses. I heard a thump and saw Cort fall behind. The arrow was through his throat and even though he tried to ask I couldn't bring him with us. He'd be dead in a minute anyway. I got to the horses first and climbed up but I waited. I counted through the men. Fin was gone. Cort was gone. Andrew and Len were with Garrison but I'd only seen Garrison. And he was the only one that stumbled through.

"Where are the others?" I said. He was staggering and I noticed the red blood pouring from his left side. But that wasn't the worst part. His cheek was flayed open from below his eye to under his chin. It just missed anything important but it was an awful, bloody sight.

Garrison wouldn't be able to ride alone. I rode over and reached down with my hands. I needed both of them to pull him behind me. "Where are they?" I asked getting nervous. We were losing our head start.

"Everyone is dead. Fin. Cort. Andrew. Len. Get out of here. We need to get out of here," he said slumping against me. I shooed our other horses free and we ran. My soul glided with us.

"They aren't following. The death of their leader was a blow. We should be okay. I'll keep scanning ahead. I let you know what's coming. I'm sorry, Derek. I shouldn't have left last night," my soul said.

"No, I'm sorry," I said and Garrison heard me, too.

"I forgive you," he said slumping against my back as his blood soaked my shirt. I wish he'd cursed me. I wish he'd reached for my dagger and slit my throat. Forgiveness. What was I supposed to do with that?

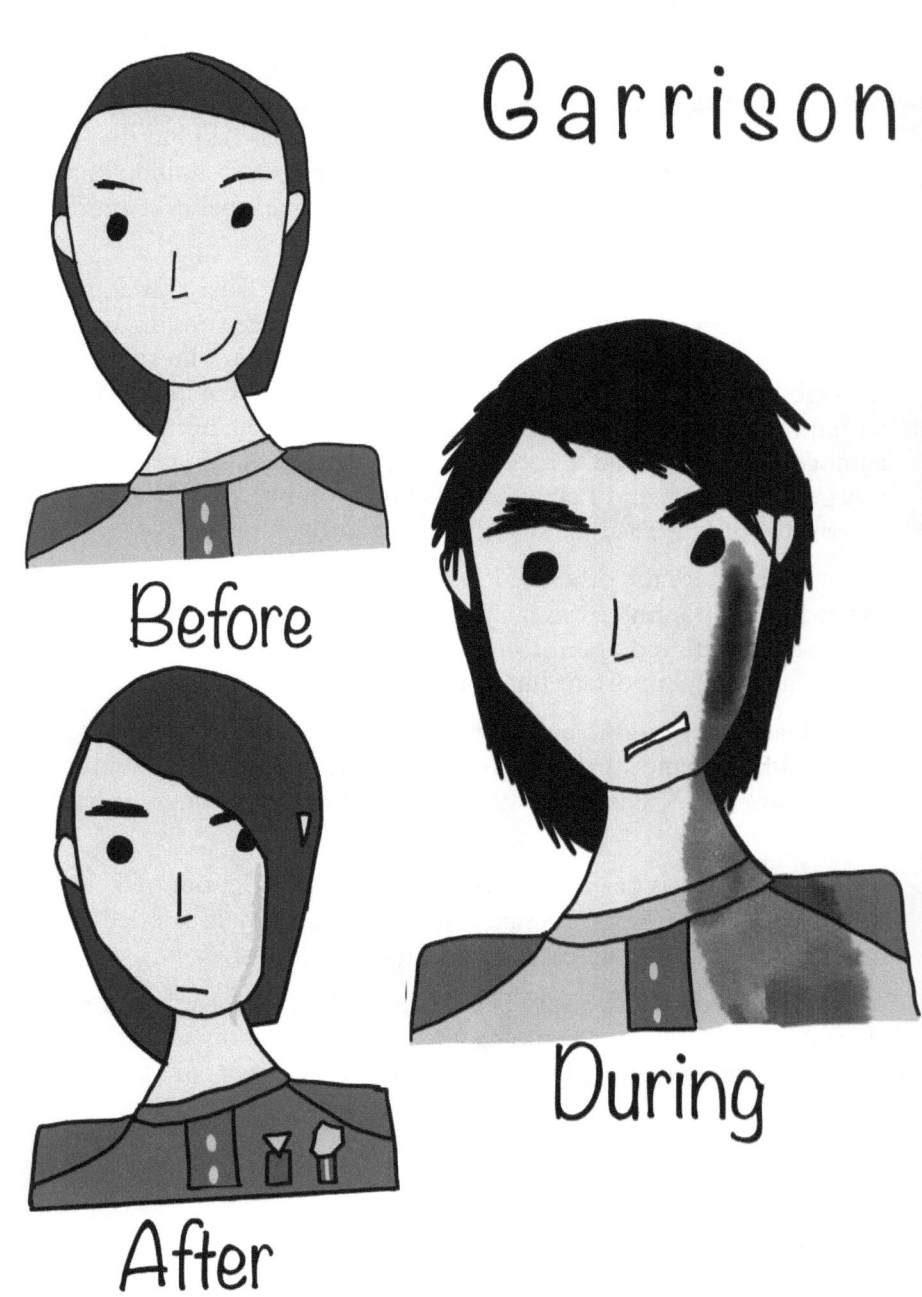

Garrison

Before

During

After

Garrison lived and his forgiveness stuck but I couldn't... I... I don't know. I was different after that. The fire of competition was completely smothered. I didn't even want it anymore. I'd lost the taste for everything. I tried to have my rank lowered but our mission had been technically a success. It didn't matter that Len, Cort, Andrew, and Fin had died because we'd discovered the identity of the men and killed their leader. Three troops were dispatched to clean up our mess as soon as I'd given our report.

Garrison was treated by the Citadel physician but the scar could not be minimized. It was enough that he could see, smell, and talk. His vanity had taken a shot but my whole identity was lost. It was *humiliating* that I'd escaped with little more than bruises and scrapes. When I tell this to Brigitte a couple years later, she'll tell me that it was the Goodness's protection. She believes in the old religion, hell if I know why. But it wasn't anyone's *kind* protection. If anything it was the Darkness preserving me for what was to come.

Our 'daring mission' promoted both of us and we were awarded medals for our fallen troop. Hezekiah and the Mage both came. I had to force myself to look them in the eye.

"Well done," Jol said and I almost heard the subtext. 'Well done for not dying and disgracing me'. I nodded and moved on.

Hezekiah clasped my shoulder but his eyes were dark. He must have read my whole report. I'd been too honest when I'd stumbled into the General's office covered in other people's blood. Amazingly his assistant let me through. That was probably due to fear. There had been a fire and darkness raging beneath my skin. It was all my fault and I told him so. I told him every detail about my failure as their leader.

"It may be true, the story you tell," the General said. "But one thing is clear. You accomplished your task amazingly well despite the severe odds against you. If you had returned home, they might have hidden again and we'd be no closer to knowing the truth. You may feel, in the light of your losses, that you led poorly but I see a man who served the Queen and killed her enemies. Well done, Derek. I see that my son did not waste his time." And I was dismissed.

His son seemed to be struggling to find the words so I started.

"I don't deserve these medals. I did nothing honorable. I was a blind fool. I failed you." The words were so honest and raw that it surprised both of us. I remember my childish goal with perfect clarity. *I want to be your equal. And I wanted to be my own master.* I was neither of those things.

He nodded his head and said "If you feel that way, then we should talk again. I've not given up on you, Derek. This more than anything shows your potential." Potential for what? Potential as nothing more than a reckless sword that swings at everything with no regard for allies or as a dishonored bitter man without hope. Either way it raised my alerts but not enough obviously

From left to right:
Garrison, Andrew, Len, Fin, Cort, and Derek

The Darkness

1

The Darkness and the Goodness. Children's tales.

Once upon a time there was a light that shone over all Morland. It protected and defended the people of the land. Those who worshiped the light were kind, brave, and good. They were strong in righteousness. They dedicated their lives to the service of the Goodness, that was what they had named the light. But the night was jealous of the people's adoration and started to leak his influence stronger and stronger. Night became more than a time of day. It became an entity, the Darkness. Those who were seduced became cruel, violent, and ambitious always seeking more and more power. The Goodness tried to restore the lost ones but it was too late. The Darkness's poison has no antidote. So a battle raged against light and dark, good and evil.

Typical of Morland, there is no happy ending to that horrible children's story. It ends with the vague lines "One day the Darkness with fail. The Darkness cannot abide the light. Goodness will shine forever."

That's all you get.

Sorry there is an everlasting war between good and evil but one day it will be over. No timeline. No details. No comfort. Why would a person choose to believe that stupid fairytale?

Now, I know a thing of two about wars and fighting and there is no big *mystical* battle going on. I haven't seen any angels and demons duking it out for control of Morland. There is only the Darkness and the Queen. Those two things I am sure of.

If there *was* a battle, the Goodness had already lost long before I came to Morland. Because the Goodness was definitely not still around and the Darkness was unbeatable. It wasn't as shocking to me as I'm sure it would have been to a normal person to be thrust into a world with a visible palpable force of evil covering the whole planet. I'd thought the sepia hue was a smog or something at first. I would never have guessed that it was a physical manifestation of an evil entity. It still sounds stupid but it's true.

The Darkness is real and I've felt it.

Once upon a time
there was a light
but the darkness destroyed it.

The End

2

Morland may have had some magic but it wasn't a fairy land for a lot of reasons. The biggest was the Darkness. It sounds like a children's story. The Darkness versus the Goodness. I don't know if there is any 'goodness' left but I've seen the Darkness and it's seen me.

The Darkness fell on the land over the course of a day they said, the day *she* came. I wasn't there, of course. This all started seventy years ago. I spoke to several older people who remembered it. They said it settled like a fog. That suddenly the colors weren't as bright. That flowers didn't smell as sweet. But wasn't that what every generation said to the next? That *they* had been the ones that really had it good. That nowadays something was broken. But maybe in this situation it was true.

The whole planet had suddenly had a haze, a brown haze, that covered everything and everyone. People eventually got used to the ill feeling that stayed in the pits of their stomachs. It became noise in the background, almost unnoticeable until they found themselves faced with the true undiluted form. There was no ignoring *that*. It was staggering. There was no denying something was wrong then.

The presence was evil. It was a malevolent force that scourged the land. When I came to Morland I had noticed it slowly. My memories of Earth quickly started to feel like dreams. Did Earth not have a haze covering the planet? Probably not. The Darkness was not just a sepia filter. It was a force. I've felt the full force of its malevolent presence plenty of times. It's hard to put into words...

The presence of the Darkness was everywhere but usually only a thin layer. But it could concentrate itself in places and then it felt like breathing in radioactive smog that made you feel ill and irritated, at least at first. Amazingly, once I was living in the castle I just got used to it. What does that say about me?

My soul told me that he saw *things* in the Darkness. Creatures that poured in and then disappeared. Things of blackness and smoke with claws as big as his head. He stayed away from them. The creatures existed in the same plane as my soul did. Somewhere a degree removed from the world of the living. I couldn't see the creatures but I didn't doubt him. They scared him and nothing scared him.

The world had been broken for seventy plus years. Ever since... Ever since she came. The Queen. I had trouble finding the truth about what happened. People didn't like to talk about it but they would after enough drink. It was like they had watched a horrible car accident. I could almost see the details replaying behind their eyes. Eventually I heard enough to piece it together.

The land had been putty to her fingers and she changed the rules like a girl changes dresses on her dolls. First came the smog of Darkness. Then she announced herself with kidnappings. A person here. A person there. At first it looked random until the pattern emerged. The Queen wanted everyone with magic running in their blood. That's when the people started to fight back.

That first generation, the grandparents of today's youths, tried to rally a rebellion. They still remembered the light. They remembered it was called the Goodness. It would surely save them if they put their trust in it. But they failed. She subjugated the whole country under her dictatorship. And then instead of taking a couple people with magic, she took *all of them* and they never came home.

I had thought about that a long time. I chewed it over in my mind. Because I had never seen a trace of all the people she had taken even when I was a prince and the castle was my home. What had she done with them? It stayed unanswered in my mind for a while. If only I'd never known the full truth of it.

The people of Morland settled under her thumb. Their last hopes crushed; they could only bow. Their beloved Goodness hadn't saved them and eventually the Goodness became a bitter poison. The power that could have saved them but instead left them to suffer under her ruling. Or maybe the Goodness was never powerful enough to help even if it wanted to. But as the years passed most finally realized that the Goodness had never existed at all. It must have just been the rallying banner for the revolution, an idea to get the masses to aid in the battle. Because if people believed the force of light was on their side then there was no danger of losing.

I can see the cold dread that fills the people now. What if there was no force of light? Maybe it was just the ever-growing Darkness and that was all there was. Maybe it would be like this forever.

I had trouble believing there was meaning to anything. It was what it was. And if there had ever been anything good in the world... I had probably killed it.

I used to try to blame who I was on the Darkness in the air. Maybe I wasn't really a bad person, deep down. Maybe I was just reacting to the presence of evil, like how a person slowly mutates in a radiation field. It wasn't *my* fault. I was just being turned into something I wasn't against my will, surely. Don't worry I didn't really believe that.

I knew I was mean. But I kind of forgot what it was like to be nice so I didn't really notice it in myself. My soul did and Garrison did. And I tried to listen to them. When I felt my stubbornness and anger rising, one look at Garrison's scar would throw a bucket on the inferno growing inside me. I'd done that.

He started to wear his black hair long to cover the worst of his scar. It didn't help. It didn't draw any less attention. My soul said that he did it because of me.

"What? Why? What do I care if he's not as pretty?" I said.

"It's not that, stupid. He knows that it makes you feel bad when you look at him. He does it to help you," my soul said. It floored me. It floored me that Garrison could be so much better than I was. If the situation had been reversed, I'd have hated him. I'd have worn my scar like a badge of hate. I'd have made him feel bad at every turn. His grace about it turned my stomach. So I stayed away. It was easy since Hezekiah had started to meet with me again.

At first it had been to discuss the incident. He wanted to know everything I told his father and everything I'd held back. I couldn't have denied his order to do so, he was second in command under his father, the General, but I didn't want to hide the truth. It felt good to let it all out. Then the questions took a turn.

"Are you happy?" he asked one night over ales. We weren't at the Starlight. Hezekiah would never go to a place like that and I didn't go there often anymore. We were at a pub called the East Gate.

Was I happy? His question startled me. Who cared if I was happy? And was *anyone* happy? I'd never met anyone who was. Garrison put on a good show with a smile and his charm but he was as broken as I was.

"No," I said without hesitation. "Are you?"

"No," he answered. "Do you think you could ever be happy?"

"No," I said just as quickly. As long as my feet were planted on Morland soil, I could never be happy. And probably not even if I was home.

"Things are changing," he said. "Subtle changes. Have you noticed?"

I nodded. It wasn't just the boldness of the nomads in speaking against her, it was the shock of what we'd found on that mission. Soldiers turned criminal, killing citizens, and daring to stand against the Queen. No one could stand against her. Her reach was strong and her magic was stronger. It was just absolute foolishness to think there was another path but to serve her. Better to be her sword killing others than the idiot being mowed down.

"And?" he said.

"And what?" I didn't know what he wanted. Who cared if idiots were risking their own necks? Morland would beat them back to a bent knee and a bowed neck. It wasn't really my concern. I was an instrument just waiting to be pointed. I tried not to think about things.

"And what are you going to do about it? Things are changing. Which side will you be on? Mine?"

"What other side is there?"

He smiled and that must have been the answer he was expecting. Maybe this was a test of loyalty. I wondered if he was tasked with checking all troop leaders for loyalty to the crown. I'd passed, I guessed.

4

What I assumed Hezekiah knew, and time would show very well that he didn't, was that his father, the General, was also testing me. But his test was more specific. He wanted to know how loyal I was to the Mage and that took a moment's thought.

"I won't beat about the bush," the General said. "The Mage trusts you."

I nodded my head. Sure. He could think that. I had no evidence to support that idea. I'd seen the Mage twice a year for the past four years. So eight visits. But that practically made Jol and I best friends with how little he suffered everyone else on the planet.

"I'm not accustomed to lending my men to do the Mage's dirty work but this army is to serve Morland and the Queen however best it can. But before I release you to him..." he said studying me. "Would you kill the Mage? If he was a danger to the Queen and all of Morland, if it was found that he was guilty of treason could you put aside your loyalty and kill him?"

"Yes," I said. But I hadn't ever thought about. I would later. I've thought about killing Jol many times. It all just kind of feels like it's his fault from my view point at the end. It's probably not. He doesn't care enough about me to do me wrong but yeah I probably could have killed him then or at least tried, if the situation had called for it.

"Good," he said dismissing me. But before I left the room he said, "And this is a solo mission. Your troop stays here under your second."

Three months ago that would have had me fuming but I knew Garrison wouldn't take advantage of my absence, even if I wished he would.

Jol was waiting for me with two horses. I nodded my head as I headed into the bunks. I grabbed my pack and weapons. Those were the only things I owned in the world.

Garrison wasn't around so I didn't get to tell him I'd be leaving. He would have just followed us, so it was for the best.

I loaded my horse and was in the saddle without a word to or from Jol. Yeah, we were *really* close. He kicked his horse and I followed him. I'd only been to Jol's house once, when I'd been recovering from my concussion before Jol had enlisted me. It was the same: kitchen, living room, bedroom. No artifacts to distinguish who lived there. Nothing remarkable at all. He lived a day's ride from the castle, half a day if you booked it. And though it was probably inconvenient when the Queen needed him, I envied his seclusion and freedom. There wasn't another house in sight. This was what I dreamed about.

"What's the plan, sir?" I said as I followed him inside.

"Drop the 'sir'. It's Jol,"

"Alright, *Jol*. What's the plan?"

"All business now. I hardly see the scared child in you anymore."

"Well that was the goal, was it not? I've grown up. I'm not scared of anything now."

"Everyone is scared of something," he said scoffing as he turned to make some tea. There he was. That scoff felt a little bit like coming home. But I was pretty sure I wasn't scared of anything. Famous last words, right? That's what fools say who don't know what they have to lose. But I never said I wasn't a fool.

"How are you?" Jol asked once the kettle was boiling over his instantly made magic fire. After four years in Morland, Jol was still the only mage I'd ever met. Beside the Queen, of course. But I hadn't met her yet. I'd seen her but we hadn't *met* yet.

"I'm okay, Jol," I said and I had to stop myself from being more honest. Jol wasn't my father. He didn't actually care about me. And I was *okay*, in a sense. I was fed and unwounded. That was my definition of 'okay' now.

He nodded absently and handed me a cup of tea. I hated his tea but it was a warm thing to drink and winter was thick in the air.

"There is a movement rising against the Queen. Talk about destroying her and freeing the world from the Darkness. It's a small movement right now but it's gaining. And I think it's being led by a mole in the Citadel," Jol said.

I almost dropped my cup.

"People are such idiots," I said out loud.

"Yes, they are," he said with almost amusement in his eyes.

"So how do we smoke him out?" I asked drinking the bitter drink and then groaned. Jol's tea was the worst.

"No wavering? You wouldn't want to see the Queen overrun?"

"Why does everyone keep testing me? Do I have a disloyal face? I don't bloody well care who is in charge. It makes no difference to my life. What would make a difference is a civil war. Things are cozy for me now. I get to drink a lot and eat a lot and spend most of my days camping under the stars. Things can only get worse and I'd prefer if they could just stay the same kind of awful. I've never met the Queen. I don't care for her but I also don't want to die in a coup. So if this thing can be stopped quickly better for me. Is that good enough, Mage? Do I pass the test?"

He rolled his eyes. That was as comforting as a hug.

"Who do you suspect?" I asked forcing myself to finish the cup. I'd feel warmer afterwards but man, it was terrible.

"Hezekiah."

I spit the whole mouthful in Jol's face.

I knew it couldn't be true but there was no convincing Jol of anything and I wasn't going to get any information out of him either. He was a boulder when you wanted to get information out of him.

"I won't tell you my source!" Jol said slamming his fist down. I could still get under his skin so easily.

"Fine," I said. "I'll figure it out either way. But you are wrong."

"We'll see," he said.

In the end, it was too bloody easy. I'd almost groaned aloud when Hezekiah told me he had some *people* he wanted me to meet. I'd hoped that if by some strange trick he was guilty then it would be months or even a year until I found him out but it only took two more of our 'talks' until he brought me along to his rebellion club's meeting place.

Oh, Hezekiah. Why did you have to be such an idiot? How could you have ever thought it would work in your favor? The General must have been suspicious. Maybe he doubted Jol. Or maybe he even knew Jol's suspicion. Maybe my chat with the General was his veiled threat that I should kill Jol if Hezekiah was found guilty. But I'm really too thick for that. I don't play mind games or any kind of games. If that was what he'd wanted he should have spelled it out and I would have agreed. I'd have chosen Hezekiah over Jol in that instant.

"We'll attack the South Coast first and cripple her fleet. Then we'll burn and pillage every major town. The Citadel will go first. We need to weaken her men and reduce the numbers," Hezekiah said with a glint in his eyes and a determined smile to his lips.

Those 'numbers' were my comrades. Those 'numbers' included Garrison. Those 'numbers' were just lost young men like me who were trying to earn a living and keep their heads off the chopping block.

And the South Coast was the best bleeding part of Morland. The ocean was the only thing that reminded me of home in a way that didn't hurt too much. Hezekiah wanted to do more destruction and harm than the Queen had done in fifty years.

Before the trap was sprung, I did try to spare him from it.

"Hezekiah, I know you want to change things. But this plan... This plan is madness. So many innocent people. So much unnecessary..."

But I was cut off. "Unnecessary? Derek, every drop of blood spilled will be a paving stone to the new Morland. A Morland free of tyranny. Think of what your life would be like free of the Queen."

The problem was that at that point it would have made no difference. My only trade was warcraft. But later... Oh I'm fate's bloody fool. I had my chance and I threw it away. But honestly, they would have failed. I didn't know specifically why they would have failed like I do now but they didn't stand a one in a trillion chance of winning against her. No one does.

That meeting was crashed by a raid of twelve troops and the General himself. I knew he wouldn't believe me if I'd told him. Hell, I didn't even want to believe myself. There was a moment as Hezekiah drew his sword, a moment where his frantic eyes found my face...

With all the blood I've shed and wrong I've done somehow this look makes the list of things that haunt me. I'd betrayed my master but not before he'd betrayed me. Or so I told myself. Hezekiah was killed in the siege and that was a good thing. It spared the General from having to dispense judgment on his only son. Instead he executed every guilty man and woman and gave me the honor of sending me far away.

Garrison was mad about it.

"You saved the bloody world and we are getting sent on tax collecting missions on the other side of the mountain. This is ridiculous. You should be the new number two," Garrison said as our troop left the Citadel for our new mission of being-the-hell-outta-the-General's-sight-forever. We were being sent away with a fresh new troop and I didn't even want to learn their names.

"He was his son," I said not turning around. "He was also my friend." And I'd betrayed him. It's apparently what I do. Hezekiah was a fool for ever imagining that the Darkness could be removed from Morland. I mean how could it when it lived in every heart?

"Darkness in every heart."

I wish I didn't agree with Derek about this. But I do...

Becoming a Prince

1

I remember the first time I saw her, the Queen. I was fourteen and little in awe. She was beautiful but like a kiss with a fist or like how a deadly viper is mesmerizing right before it unhinges its jaw and lunges. It was disconcerting to know how long she'd looked that way. Seventy years of unchanging youth. But the trick to noticing that something was wrong was to look in her eyes. There was a darkness there, a blackness that sent chills up my spine.

Her hair was long and black and she'd had it braided simply down her back as she'd addressed her army. She'd do that periodically, show her face. It was good for us to remember her and to remember to be afraid. The Darkness coalesced into a thick cloud and I *felt* afraid. But I'd only been a kid then. The next several times I saw her were just as fleeting and unsettling. People really didn't talk about her much, not until the tournament started with its monthly competitions.

Once a month, starting shortly after I turned seventeen, there was a competition that was held as a part of a larger tournament at the castle. Of course we weren't there, my troop and I were as far from the castle as was possible in Morland. We were charting and collecting taxes on the other side of the mountain and getting bored out of our minds. But it was nice thinking that I hadn't killed anyone in a while.

We received updates via town gossip and letters. When one missive told us to make our way back, Garrison was absolutely thrilled. My soul and I were less so. It had been good for us to be away. My soul was still a little sick about the Hezekiah incident. He had disliked spying on our master and friend. He'd agreed with me at the end but he still wasn't happy about it. Being alone in the wilderness was good for him. But no rest for the wicked, right?

We made it back to the castle in the middle of the seventh month of the tournament and the next competition event was to be held at the end of the month like it had ben the previous seven months.

The Queen had chosen one person each month for the past six months and the winner's life was completely changed. Whoever won that month's competition was legally adopted by the Queen and became a prince or princess of Morland.

I had no desire to win. Especially when the first month's news brought the name of the winner. Even Garrison was momentarily turned off to the idea of winning.

"Felix won?" he asked reading over my shoulder. "Are you sure it was him? Maybe it was a different one." It wasn't.

Felix was five years older than Garrison and I. He was twice as wide and thick as the two of us combined. He had brown hair that he kept short and dark brown eyes that made even me look away in submission. He was... not the kind of person I'd thought was real. I'd met many awful characters upon arriving in Morland but I still had thought some villains were only pretend. But Felix was very much alive and real, unfortunately.

I'd instinctively known to avoid him, like how kids know the rules of the playground without being told. There are parts you just can't use because the big kids hang out over there. It was like that but more. Felix raised my hackles and that was before I even knew him. I'd thought I was cruel but Felix made me look like a saint.

We had our first interaction when I was fifteen and he was twenty. It was our first big mission and we were being chaperoned by Felix's troop. I didn't like the idea of being watched by him and his buddies but we didn't get a say. The week before we left my soul did a couple days of reconnaissance on Felix and what he brought back was disturbing.

"The facts," he said sitting across from me on our bunk. That wasn't a good start. That meant we were facing a problem. I adjusted my position unnecessarily and nodded at him to continue. "First, he's an alcoholic. For real. When he's sober, he's angry and short-temped but unfortunately he's rarely sober. Because when he's drunk he's violent, cruel, and furious. But in a cold way, like a cold fury. Like how you get sometimes but times a million."

It was weird to have my soul spell out my faults. I knew he knew what they all were but we usually just pretended he didn't notice what a monster I was. But 'monster' was about to get a more complete definition.

"Second?" I asked.

"Second, he's an asshole. Third, he always smells. Always. Like a semester-old gym bag that's been thrown up in and soaked with piss. It's pleasant. You are gonna love it." I rolled my eyes and he continued.

"Fourth, he... I said he's violent but I think you need an example. You know how the older guys have servants to help with their laundry and meals and stuff."

"Yeah."

"Okay, so yesterday a maid is bringing in his uniforms. And Felix checks his clothes but a belt is missing. So he grabs her arm hard, hard enough to make her cry out. He asks her nice and calm when his belt is. She says that it must have fallen out while she was coming up the stairs and that she'll go look for it or get him a new one. He says that it's too late for that. He throws her around a bit and... you can guess. He told her that if she told on him he'd kill her and her whole family. I believe him. So... our goal for this trip is to be invisible. He's going to find someone to pick on. Don't. Let. It. Be. You. Derek, *please*. Don't let him bait you or make you mad. Be invisible and not worth his time."

I nodded. I could do that. I could probably do that. I'd try my very best to do that. I gave Garrison a heads up and he thankfully agreed with me. Our competitive spirit had not yet blossomed into the destructive force it would turn into. But Felix didn't give any of us a second glance. He had other things on his mind.

The town of Bentcreek was small but really beautiful. There was a large creek than ran through town and it was as picturesque as the puzzles my mom liked to do. I remember when we crossed a hill and saw the whole town in one view that I wanted to live there. It seemed like it wasn't even a part of Morland but it was. And I haven't ever been back there.

Our mission was to investigate a family harboring a child with magic. I guess I should explain. We did three jobs as the Queen's men: collected taxes, kept people too afraid to rebel, and hunted down people with magic. I hadn't caught anyone with magic yet. There really weren't that many mages.

The Queen's magicide decades ago had done wonders. But we had a strong feeling that this time it wasn't a hoax. There had been strange weather, snow in the summer, rain every day at the same time and other stuff like that. When we caught the mage, we were to take him to the castle and he'd disappear just like all the rest. I didn't *love* the idea of finding one.

Felix stormed into the town like a villain from the Old West. People peeked around doors and windows. "Bring him out," Felix said as we stood in the middle of the small town square.

It didn't take long for Felix to break the truth out of someone. The mage we were looking for was a child. He couldn't have been ten. My feet started moving before I knew what I was doing. Garrison hissed and my soul stood in my path like he could stop me. But even if he couldn't physically touch me, it jarred me out of myself.

Thankfully, Felix hadn't noticed but my feet were itching to stop whatever was coming. The young mage's parents begged for leniency and as the boy got scared a storm cloud started to form above us.

Felix didn't hesitate.

He pulled his sword free and cut the parents down as he said completely professionally, "You stand against the Queen and Morland. Harboring a mage is a capital offense. Your punishment is death." He said it like he was reading someone the Miranda rights. "You have the right to remain silent..." He then took the butt of his sword and nailed the screaming child on the side of the head instantly turning off the storm overhead. Then after a kick to the stomach, he hoisted the kid onto his horse like he was a bag of potatoes.

Two townsfolk men stepped forward with small daggers that looked more like shearing knives than attack weapons and one said "Give the boy back. He's never hurt anyone."

A smile crossed Felix's face. He gave the reigns of his horse to his number two, Joseph, and then strolled toward the men. He struck them down with the same apathy and cold words but this time there was a light in his eyes. "You stand against the Queen and Morland. Harboring a magician is a capital offense. Your punishment is death." Then he added with a smirk, "Anyone else?" No one else stepped forward and Felix shrugged.

We started to leave and then Felix turned back. "Go ahead, Joseph. I'll catch up with you in a bit." I don't know how many more people he killed. I didn't turn around when I heard the screaming start.

Thankfully, I didn't throw up until I was alone on watch that night. The kid was kept drugged with some awful smelling water the whole trip to the castle. I was glad when I wasn't invited to present him to the Queen. Garrison and I never talked about that trip and we never had to go on another trip with Felix's men because they were all promoted and too busy to babysit newbies.

So when I heard that the Queen had chosen to adopt Felix and in doing so gave him the title and power of "Prince". I could not have been more turned off to the idea. When we returned to the Citadel after a long time gone, I was very glad to receive Jol's message to come help with an errand. I was more than willing to be a day away from the action but it didn't last long, of course.

2

I hadn't intended on entering the tournament. I wasn't even supposed to be in the Capitol that day. Jol had me running errands all over the woods. Since I'd been back from my exile he'd taken more of an interest in me. Maybe because I'd shown him loyalty in the whole Hezekiah disaster or maybe I was finally enough of a man to be worth his time. I don't know but it was nice to have a distraction. Jol tried to keep me too busy to look for my stupid tree. He told me I'd never find it and even if I did, he didn't expect it would do anything.

I'd ventured closer to the road than I'd planned and Garrison found me. "What are you doing out here? It starts at noon," he said scanning the trees to gauge the time.

"Yeah, I wasn't going to go. I'd already promised Jol I'd help him out with some things today," I said.

He rolled his eyes. "I don't know why you spend time with the old man. And who cares what you promised him you'd do. Nothing else matters today except the tournament. This is the last competition, they say. We've both been gone on patrols for ages and we missed the first six competitions but not this one. You are coming with me and one of us is going to win."

Garrison was less than pleased with my blank expression.

"Deeerrrreeeeekkk!" he grounded dragging my name out several syllables. "Come on! Isn't this everyone's dream? You wouldn't have to work or travel for weeks in the pouring rain, sharing your tent with stinky Jeffery. We've seen a lot of this stupid country and the capital is the best place. And you could be its bloody prince. Who doesn't want that? I mean, I'll be entering so you won't actually get to be a prince but I'd appreciate the audience," Garrison said smiling. His scar moved only when he smiled. It ran the length of his face and he had finally stopped covering it with his long dark hair. I should have felt guilty when I looked at it but it just reminded me of all the trouble we'd gotten into over the years and I couldn't help but smile.

He'd won. "Aha! There he is. Welcome back. Come on. Watch me become the last prince."

After we'd been riding for a couple minutes, he turned suddenly and grabbed my arm. "It's actually our manly duty to win. Do you realize the last winner was a girl? Ha. No girl is taking the spot this time. I can't believe two have won already. Nope. It's gonna be one of us."

Oh, Garrison. How many times did I selfishly, horribly wish you had won instead of me?

The competition was sword fighting. Apparently every month had been a different sort of contest. "I bet last month was a floor sweeping contest," Garrison murmured once we were both in line waiting our turn. I looked around for my soul, wondering where he'd been today. He really was his own man coming and going when he pleased. I liked it best when he was with me. Sometimes my head was so foggy when he was gone that I was unable to decide what I should do. Not that I'd ever told him that. I'd never live it down.

Turning to the right I saw *them* for the first time. Six imposing figures sitting around to the Queen on the stage. It sent a shiver down my spine. I'd seen the Queen before, of course. She wasn't the sort to just sit hidden in her chambers all day. But she was more intimidating today with all of them with her. I felt all of their eyes on me like daggers and they weren't even looking at me.

There were three filled seats on each side of her and I didn't like to look at the empty seat on the far right. On her left were three young men. I only knew the first one, Felix.

If the Queen wanted people like Felix... I didn't want anything to do with her. The Queen's army attracted all sorts and I wasn't actually the worst kind. I didn't know the other two guys but everyone was talking about them and I soon picked up information on all of them.

The one next to Felix was Gabriel. He was tall and thin with blond hair to his shoulders and a manicured short beard. He wore glasses and seemed to be weighing and evaluating every competitor one by one. His eyes were roaming and calculating settling for a moment on each man and woman in the crowd before moving to the next.

Beside Gabriel was Riley. He had thick brown hair that he couldn't stop running his hands through as he mental undressed every woman who passed by. The women who had already met him wore sneers laced with fear and the many, many who hadn't met him yet stared back with open excitement.

The Royal Family

Felix

Gabriel

Riley

The Queen

Milena

Jermaine

Brigette

???

Sitting on the Queen's right was the most beautiful woman I'd ever seen and she was well aware of that fact. Milena had long auburn hair and was thin and womanly at the same time. She caught my glance as I assessed her and she rolled her eyes, dismissing me instantly. Which was fine, I'd lost my taste for women like her.

Next to her was Jermaine and I could have sworn he was a West nomad. But that was impossible. Relations with the nomads were more than a *little* tense. He had tan skin and dark hair and from his apathy he could have been anywhere doing anything.

Next to him was Brigitte. She was the one who had won the competition last month. She wasn't as beautiful as the other woman but she was arresting. She looked like a Southie, the dark skinned nomads from the South Coast. Her skin was the color of rich sweet earth and her eyes were a golden brown. I can still see her sitting there when I close my eyes. She was bored out of her mind and I found that comforting. She was the only one of the six that seemed like a normal human.

Seeing them all sitting by the Queen, silent and imposing, made me really not want to be there anymore. I was just about to make an excuse to Garrison when the trumpets started and the castle guards grouped us into sparing sets and then it all happened so fast.

I know I couldn't have been the best swordsman that day. I'd only been training for a couple years and most of them had probably first held a sword at age five. But when I finished my sparing and stole a glance up on the stage, I knew she'd picked me. I knew with certainty as my veins filled with ice.

I can still feel that moment. The memory is so sharp and preserved. The rest of the crowd wouldn't know for another hour and I felt every second of it. I purposefully kept my back to her after that, drinking as much as I could with the coins I had. Garrison was very amused.

"That bad, huh?" he laughed hitting me on the back too forcefully causing me to spit out a mouthful of precious distraction.

"Hey, watch it," I barked, taking a big gulp to replace the lost one.

"I thought you did fine," he said subdued. "You won your match. I won too," he said puffing out a little. "Which you would have seen if you hadn't decided to drink all the ale in the whole country in one sitting."

"I shouldn't have come today. Oh God!" I said slamming my hands into my forehead. "I know I will regret today. Where is he?" I said nervously scanning the crowd. I felt frantic without my soul. Where had he been? If he'd been here, he would have stopped me. He would have been that voice telling me what to do.

"Where is who?" Garrison said trying to follow my gaze. "Are you alright? Are you getting sick? Maybe I should take you somewhere to lie down."

Garrison started pulling me up as the trumpets blared. I promptly vomited on his shoes. He let out some choice curses and then pulled me up. "Well you'll probably feel better now at least."

One of the chief capitol guards said a few words which I didn't hear until he said my name "Derek of the forty-second unit." Garrison's mouth might have fallen all the way to the floor. Thankfully, I did feel slightly better since vomiting on his shoes.

I started walking towards the front when *he* finally showed up. I shouldn't have even looked at my soul but I couldn't stop myself. I wanted to see him as he saw the whole disaster that might have been avoided if he had been there. He was so pale and the horror on his face was exactly what I felt. I shrugged my shoulders at him as if to say 'Yeah, so what? It's too late now.'

I climbed up the steps and the Queen spoke just loud enough for me to hear. "To your new life," she said handing me a goblet. I drank the whole thing in one drink. She smiled and pulled me down as she kissed my forehead and whispered "Welcome home, last born."

And it seemed as if I could almost see the chains that I felt wrapping around my wrists, ankles, and neck.

3

I wasn't permitted to even return to the Citadel for my things. They'd be brought to my new room, I was told. My soul didn't leave my side as we were led deep into the castle. There was to be a ball that night in honor of my 'homecoming'. It all just felt like some crazy mistake.

"Here is your room, my prince," the guard said depositing me at a plain door and bowing his head as he left. *My prince*. It sent shivers up my spine. I looked at my new room and was impressed.

I'd never had my own room. The barrack at the Citadel had been packed to the max. I almost didn't know what to do without the hustle and noise of dozens of men. But it was nice and I wasn't really alone.

"Alright," my soul said sitting down and nodding his head down to indicate I was to copy him. "What the hell happened? I'm gone for a couple hours and you are a flipping bloody prince." My soul rarely curses. So it's an indication of how pissed he is that he said 'hell' and 'bloody' but being the goody-two shoes he is I should also count 'flipping'.

"Three curse words. Watch it soul," I said laughing. He wasn't laughing and I wasn't really either. "I don't know. It happened so fast. Garrison corrals me into going to the competition." My soul rolls his eyes so dramatically I can almost hear it.

"Of course," he says nodding for me to continue, "Cause we have to do whatever Garrison says."

"I didn't think much of it. I had no idea she'd pick me. I was not the best there. I know it. Garrison and I are tied and there were soldiers much more talented than us trying out. I don't know, soul. I don't know but she picked me. I could feel it. I just knew when she looked at me. And where were you? Why weren't you there? You could have stopped me. You could have told me what to do!" I yelled. I would have been spitting in his face if he and I were in the same plane.

"Ha!" he barked. "Like you ever listen to me. Ever! That's a joke. This is *your* fault. My being there does nothing to stop this. You do what you want to do. The only thing that would be different right now is that I'd be saying 'I told you so' instead of 'what were you bloody thinking, you absolute idiot?' You know better than this. You are better than this. Best case scenario was that you lose but even then you are drawing attention to yourself in a public setting in front of the Queen!"

"I know. I know all that. I just... I wasn't thinking." We each took a deep breath. "What do we do now?" I asked him.

"I'll start scouting the castle," he said reluctantly. "Maybe this won't be the dumbest thing you've ever done. Maybe we can make something of this."

But he'll be wrong. It is the dumbest thing I ever did. Not the worst thing I ever did but the dumbest, stupidest choice, rivaling the tree but then I'd been a kid who didn't know what could happen. I had no excuse this time.

4

Jol didn't come to see me at the castle. I didn't expect him to but I did wonder what he thought about the whole mess I'd gotten myself into. A couple weeks after my 'coronation' I left the castle to pick up some things in the marketplace when Jol fell into step with me and said "How is it going, your highness?"

It took an effort not to jump at this sudden appearance. "As good as can be expected," I said meaning a lot of different things I didn't know how to articulate. "I bet you are feeling pretty happy with your investment. All your minimal effort and small amount of care have led your foundling boy into the castle. Come to get a favor?"

He didn't smile. I didn't either.

"It's done, I guess," he said as we walked not looking at each other.

Yes, it was done. But it wasn't all bad. At this early point it wasn't even a little bad. It was odd and disorienting to be a prince. I lived in a castle and had six siblings. (More on them soon). But it wasn't *bad*. I did miss having a job and a purpose and a mission. I impossibly missed Garrison a little bit. He didn't know how to be around me and it made us both uncomfortable. So he faded away and I let him.

"Did you want something?" I asked Jol. He was never one for chitchat and his clandestine meeting with me away from the castle peaked my interest… and worry.

"No… I guess not. I just want to see you and make sure that…" Jol didn't finish his thoughts. We just walked in silence. Maybe now that I was a prince I was worth Jol's time. Maybe this would be our new normal, walking silently through the city streets. I almost chuckled. Jol turned to me and found what he really wanted to say.

"You know not to talk about it," he said meeting my green eyes with his steely gray eyes. What was he thinking saying that in a crowded marketplace? There was only one thing he could mean: Earth. He didn't say anything that would mean anything to an eavesdropper but it still made me what to scan the area and speak in a whisper.

"Yes, Mage," I said shaking my head and glaring. "Despite the absurdity of my situation, I have not lost all my senses. Nothing has changed in that respect. I don't talk about it and I don't think about it. And it would be best if you did the same. I know you have kept this to yourself and I will not be the one to break the secret. Unless you have anything to tell me, let it be."

And that was that… for then at least. We weren't done talking about Earth.

My Sister

1

One moment struck me as I wrote the title of this section. It's not at the beginning of my story with her but it's so true of us and so prophetic of what goes wrong that I'm going to cheat and put it first.

"Oh, where is it?" Brigitte said as she starting rifling through my saddlebags. "What is all this rubbish? And where is my present?" Her lilting brogue was the cutest sound I knew.

I chuckled and said, "What a little snoop you are, my sister. Maybe you are too old for presents." Brigitte struck a hand to her heart with a little gasp and said "Never" as she continued to rummage. With a flourish I pulled a small package from my jacket pocket. She squealed a sound of delight and tore through the brown paper. I had gotten her a necklace with a white stone. It reminded me of my moon.

"Oh I love it," she said grinning as she fastened it. "But this hardly makes up for your being gone so long. Where do you go? I know that Mother doesn't let you ride with your old troop because it's too dangerous for her precious little last born."

"Ha Ha," I said avoiding answering. I had been looking for the way home. It was my only hobby. I hadn't found it, of course. I felt a twinge of guilt for not telling Brigitte the truth. She was the person I loved most in this world but I heeded the old Mage's advice and told no one. I did wonder if the knowledge could ever put her in danger and in truth, home was starting to look like less of a necessity and more of a bonus. I didn't hate my life anymore. Being a prince and having brothers and sisters was nice. And I hadn't expected to get Brigitte. She had become a true sister shortly after the first time we officially met.

2

The Queen had thrown a ball in my honor and I was slowly dying of boredom. The walls of the throne room were covered in floor to ceiling mirrors and it transformed the crowded room into a suffocating cacophony of noise and bodies. The idea of spending the whole evening in there made panic start to rise but I took a deep breath and squashed it down. I was good at that, at least.

A wealthy woman had been stalking me all night and I was not interested in the least. A woman like her came with strings and I had enough of those already. I *heard* Brigitte grinning before I even turned around. It sounded like coming home.

"You are being hunted," Brigitte said with humor in her eyes. Her Scottish brogue, South accent, as it was called in Morland, rolled off her tongue and surprised me. Maybe she really was a nomad.

She had won the last competition and I remembered seeing her on the stage while I dueled. Her dark skin and hair were complemented by the golden dress she wore. It made her eyes shine but in a dangerous way. I remember comparing her to a tiger. I was proud she was my sister now.

"I noticed."

"Are you interested in Slutty Priya?" she asked.

"Is that her official title?" I laughed. "I didn't know they'd made it official. And no, I am not interested."

"Good. I'd hoped you wouldn't be an idiot," she said grabbing my hand and forcing me into a dance. The look on Priya's face had been the best welcome present.

"Ready to go?" Brigitte asked as we neared the door leading to the outside veranda.

"Can we go?" I asked glancing at our mother. The word was still strange to think. The Queen had adopted me and she wanted us to call her 'mother'.

"Oh, she won't care. She just wants you to get settled in. I ditched my first dance too," she said sliding the door open and pulling me through. We were on the second floor and I wondered if she had a plan to get down when I noticed the rope tied to the balcony.

"You think ahead," I said impressed. "What would you have done if I had wanted to spend the night with the infamous Priya?"

"Then you might have found your way down without the rope," she said smiling with all her teeth. I found myself laughing a deep laugh.

"I think we are going to get along great," I said. Her dark humor was exactly like mine.

We had a picnic under the stars that she had packed with wine and desserts stolen from the ball.

"Why'd you really go to all this trouble?" I asked. No one had ever made such an effort for me.

"It's been lonely."

"It's not like you are an only child."

"It feels like it a little. I don't know why she picked me sometimes. I don't feel like I fit in."

"I'm sure they all feel like that. Even Felix hasn't been a prince for a full year."

"Felix," she said showing her teeth, "is a piece of work."

"Yeah. I met him before he was chosen. I won't give you the details but I don't even visit that town anymore. What about the others? I've been away."

"Next was Gabriel. It was a scholar competition. He reads a lot and doesn't really notice humans. He's not bad but he's a bore. Then came Riley, his competition was an archery contest. I don't like him because he hurts the women he's with. And he's just gross. And then came Milena." When she saw my face she rolled her eyes.

"Oh, she's beautiful all right but she is the most manipulative woman I've ever met. Everything is somehow wrong and everything she says means something else. She won in a baking competition. It's so cliché it kills me. Especially because I know it wasn't even her work. A scandal came out a while after by someone saying they should have won but it was quickly quieted.

"Jermaine isn't bad. His was a horse riding competition, which might be cheating because he's a Westie. You know they raise them. I once rode one of their nomad horses. It felt like flying. But he's nice enough. At least he's not an East nomad, can't understand a bloody thing they say," she said winking. East nomads had Irish accents but I made myself use the correct terms. They had East accents and Brigitte's accent wasn't Scottish but South. Misusing terms was dangerous and I tried to be vigilant.

The Tournament Timeline

Announcement

Competitions once a month

1st Competition

Wrestling
Felix

2nd Competition

Scholarly
Gabriel

4th Competition

Baking
Milena

3rd Competition

Archery
Riley

4th Competition

Horse Riding
Jermaine

6th Competition

Daggers
Brigitte

7th Competition

Swords
Derek

"Liking animals is a good thing in my book. I do actually like Jermaine even if we don't really have anything else in common," she said.

"One big happy family, huh?" I said and not for the first or last time I considered my luck. "Did you win your contest?" I asked her. It had been bugging me since in my own I clearly hadn't been the best swordsman.

"I've thought a lot about that and I think she's not looking for the winner," Brigitte said. "I did fairly well in my competition. It was a dagger throwing contest. Did you try any of the other competitions? I don't know I've ever seen you before."

"No, I didn't. I traveled a lot with my troop. We usually were in charge of the outer borders. I only just made it in time for this one. Did you try at any others?" She looked away suddenly and I didn't ask again. I found out later she'd been to each one of them. I wouldn't find out until much much later what drove her so strongly to find a new life.

"I know it's rude to ask but are you a Southie?" I asked. I'd never met one before. I'd been to the coast but the South nomads stayed at sea for most of the year.

"No. Not every dark-skinned girl with a South accent is a nomad. I was born on the coast. But I don't talk about it. So don't bring it up again." And I didn't. It wasn't hard. I had plenty of things I didn't want to talk about either.

"So what now?" I asked after a bit. The silence with her was so companionable. I almost didn't want to break it.

"Now you rest. It's a lot of time with Mother and a lot of time to pursue your own interests. And," she said grinning impishly, "it will be a lot of time trying to entertain your charming older sister."

"Is it too late to back out?" I said pretending to rise.

"Yep. We are all bonded to the Queen and each other. Can't you feel it?" she said touching my shoulder.

And I did feel it. A deepness. A kinship. Brigitte would become the best friend I ever had. I hated leaving her as often as I did but searching for the portal home was my only past time and I didn't know how I would keep it together if I gave up on it. If I decided that Morland would be my only life, I didn't know who I would be.

And of course it was my obsession with my old life that destroyed the life I was living. It destroyed Brigitte and broke the whole world. I should have stopped looking. I should have tried to make my life at the castle a great life because it was slowly becoming that. Having a sister was the greatest experience of my life. A couple of our other siblings sometimes joined our adventures but we were two peas in a pod. And when she died, I wished I was dead too.

3

Our first adventure was also our worst one. Well not really but we were still figuring each other out and Gabriel had decided to join us. Thinking back, I think he was probably a spy. Our Mother had sent him to make sure I didn't run away or do anything too stupid.

Not that I could run anywhere that she wouldn't be able to find me. Well maybe that's something we can talk about at the end. Can you run from your destiny?

So anyway there was this old tale about a magic fountain that granted wishes. You can guess why I was interested and Brigitte's eyes opened wide when I proposed the adventure as well. I didn't know what she would wish for, not yet.

Gabriel laughed.

"Are you two serious?" he asked as I explained the plan over breakfast.

"Serious as death," Brigitte said before a smart response even entered my brain. Her smile was wide and serious and I burst out laughing. She didn't even flinch.

"It's a children's tale. It's not *real*," Gabriel said slowly, trying to reason with us but we were not so easily brought to reason. "Where did you even hear about it?"

"A children's book," I said watching from the corner of my eyes as Brigitte choked on her water.

"Exactly," Gabriel said as if he had won.

"Yes, exactly," I said smiling. "There is nothing more reliable than children's tales. They are how children learn the workings and rules of the world."

"Let's hear it then," Brigitte said raising her eyebrows and nodding.

Gabriel started to tell it but I raised my hand. "No offense big brother but I've got this one. This story requires a little... panache." I said at the same time that Brigitte said "cockamamie." I huffed. Brigitte grinned. Gabriel finally rolled his eyes.

Brigitte drew a line of the table with her finger. She'd won this round. We played a lot of dumb games. One of them was to see which of us could break Gabriel first. He was always so calm and scholarly and proper but with a little ingenuity and relentlessness we could surpass even his tolerance. I nodded my head at her in respect and started the story.

"Once upon a time, there was an old man who had lost everything: his wife, his kids, his fortune and his health. He had no home and nowhere to go so he roamed Morland like a destitute man being blown by the three winds.

"One dark night as he was wandering without purpose and hope he saw a faint moonbeam shining off to the right of the road. There was a great oak tree guarding a well and he never would have seen it if not for the one stray moonbeam that had slipped through the branches.

"Now the man was very thirsty and he reached into the well to pull up the rope for the bucket but as he pulled, the rope came up easily for there was no bucket attached. The man looked all around but there was no way for him to reach the water. He wondered bitterly if there ever had been any water. It was probably just a trick. He reached down at his feet and found a stone the size of his hand and threw it into the well. He was shocked when he heard a rich deep splash. There was water and it was just out of his reach. His anguish rose up and he said 'I wish there was a bucket!'

"The man heard a clatter and looked down to see a bucket tied neatly to the end of the rope. He joyfully threw it into the well and pulled up a full bucket of water. It was the sweetest moment he had known since he had lost everything and the taste of the water drew a memory that until then had only brought him pain. He remembered a summer day when his family had taken off work in the fields to swim and play in the stream. The sun had been so warm and the water had been so cool and crisp. Before he knew what he was doing, he reached down and found another rock. He looked at it for a moment and then threw it into the well. After he heard the splash he said, 'I wish my family was alive.'

"No sooner were the words out of his mouth when he saw shadows rise before him. He looked to see his wife, his daughter, and his two sons looking just as young as they had when the fever had taken them so long ago. His head was swimming and his vision blurred. He

105

thought there must be tears falling from his eyes but it had been so long since that happened last he wasn't sure. His reached out his arms and he was finally holding his family again.

"He kissed each of their heads and felt short of breath at his good fortune to have them back again. His wife looked up at him and tried to speak but her voice was a raspy whisper. He hurried to the well and pulled up a bucket of water and his wife drank it greedily.

"Then he drew another for his daughter and she drank. Then he drew another for his first son and he drank. As he pulled up the last bucket it seemed to have gained a hundred pounds. He pulled and pulled but his muscles were weak. He finally pulled the rope the last foot and the bucket reached the top. His last son grabbed the bucket but the old man started to hack and cough and he realized that the water must not have been as pure and clean as he had thought. He hadn't been crying out of relief and he hadn't lost his breath out of joy.

"The water was bad.

"He yelled 'No!!' But his last son had already tipped the bucket back. He gathered his family together one last time in his arms and this time he died first. The End."

"What the hell kind of a story was that?" Brigitte said grinning and shaking her head. "It's literally the worst story I've ever heard. Oh Derek. That's really awful." But she chuckled. She too seemed to understood that Morland was the worst and of course that ending was the only one that could have come.

"When do we leave?" Brigitte asked. Gabriel rolled his eyes again and I groaned. Two wins!

"Ugh!" I said. "Now, I guess. You coming, big brother? We will only get more energized from the open road?"

"Someone has to keep you two children from drinking the water just to test if it is really poisoned or not. But there is no well. It's a story and nothing else. We can go look but you won't find it."

We found many wells but none protected by oak trees and none that granted wishes. Though each time Brigitte and I solemnly tossed in a rock. We didn't joke around then because when we found that well we didn't want to waste our wishes.

"You two do understand the moral of that story, don't you?" Gabriel asked on the second day, unable to keep quiet any longer. When we ignored his question he told us anyway. "The moral is twofold. The first is to be careful what you wish for. The man wishes for a bucket but it only held death and he wished for his family but they were not as they seemed. The second moral is to accept the bad things that come into our life and to rise above them."

"What do you know of bad things, Gabriel?" Brigitte bit back. "You are a tall handsome smart white man. What struggles have come your way, pray tell? What have you had to 'rise above'?"

Gabriel didn't get angry or offended. He looked straight into Brigitte's eyes and said "We were all orphans, were we not?" Brigitte eyes flashed a moment. I didn't know then but she was not an official orphan. She was in the sense that he father was dead and her mother was a monster. She was an orphan in every way that counted. And I wasn't an official orphan either but I was alone and parentless and wasn't that the definition of it.

She nodded.

"We all got to that state a different way," Gabriel said, "and I assure you there is no easy path. I do not know your road, little sister. I would listen if you would tell me. But here is mine.

"My parents died of famine. A slow, hard death. I watched as every scrap was given to me and they slowly shriveled into nothing. I watched as the mayor of the town ate and ate as he sat in his library and read book after book. One of those books was worth a month's food for my whole family and enough left over to buy two chickens.

"When my parents died, I wandered the streets not unlike our friend from the story but I was found and adopted by the mayor himself. He took me in and taught me to read and I read every one of those books. I saw that indeed they were worth keeping.

"Unfortunately, shortly after I turned sixteen the mayor had left a candle in the library and himself and the whole house burned in a flash. I barely made it out alive. Since I had received such a good education I was able to find work and support myself but I was ever alone. I could have chosen to die of starvation in that house. I could have chosen to hate the man who let my parents die. I could have chosen to die in that fire along with my beloved books. But I rose above it as have both of you. You are stronger from your hardships and struggles. You have grown into a man and woman that our Mother found worthy. We are none of us alone any more. You don't need this well. You have all you could ever need."

I nodded and Brigitte nodded but when Gabriel was asleep we both stole out to try one more well. After that one too failed us, we returned home. Gabriel's story had taken some of the fun and magic out of the adventure and had brought us back to the harsh reality of life.

4

I could write a whole book about my year with Brigitte. We had so many adventures and laughs (and hard times) but I think you'd be bored to read it. And it just might kill me to remember it all enough to write it out.

But here is another taste. Birthdays in Morland are not really a celebrated thing. Or maybe they are and I'd never had anyone who cared about me. But when my eighteenth birthday started to roll around I knew I wanted to do something to mark it. And the only person I wanted around was Brigitte.

I had been keeping my ears open for something fun and new to do when I heard about it, the Starry Ocean Festival. The South Coast had a festival every year to mark the return of the light fish. They were a kind of fish with luminescent scales that shimmered in the moonlight like silver gems.

Everyone was allowed to catch them and then there was a big cookout with food and dancing and music. There were not many festivals left in Morland and it just sounded too exciting and different to pass up. I knew that Brigitte didn't like to talk about her past and her childhood in the south but I thought a little visit wouldn't be the worst thing in the world. Yeah, I know you know enough to guess already that I will be wrong.

We left the castle with plenty of days to make it to the festival. I only informed Mother the morning we left by slipping a note under the door of her office. I didn't want our siblings to come and I didn't want to take the chance she'd say no. It wasn't that I distrusted our Mother, which I should have. I was just wary of everyone and preferred to keep my business to myself. Brigitte was very excited for our adventure like always but as our journey went more and more southward, she got testy.

"Where are we going?" she asked for the tenth time that morning alone each time progressively getting more irritated.

"Somewhere exciting!" I said. I was starting to feel like maybe returning to her home city was a bad idea but I'd kept the surprise for so long I was now clutching it as a shield to buy me time from the wrath I felt coming.

"Just tell her," my soul said. He'd been getting more and more antsy as she'd increased her huffing and arguing. "Don't be selfish. She seems really upset. Come on." I ignored him and rolled my eyes. Brigitte caught my eye roll and naturally assumed it was directed at her. She did not like this.

"Derek, I don't want to go any further," she said pulling her horse's reigns to a stop. And she just stared at me. "Derek, do you remember the conversation we had the night you became prince?"

I nodded.

This seemed to be the wrong answer because her eyes narrowed and her nostrils flared.

"Then what in the hell are we doing this far south? The only thing this way is the coast. And when we met I told you that I was from the coast and I didn't want to talk about it and I never wanted to go back. Where you not listening? Do you not care about me at all? Or did it slip out of your mind on one of your many adventures that I'm not allowed to join you on? What are we doing and where are we going? Tell me now or I'm leaving."

I felt my face flush and I saw my soul's anguish at causing her pain. He rung his hands and his eyes were pleading me to be kind. But he needn't have. I could still feel shame, a little bit at least.

"Okay," I said getting off my horse and tying the reigns to a tree. I sat down with my legs crossed and waited for her to join me. I just thought better in this position. My head cleared being a little lower to the ground. She let out one last huff and joined me on the ground with a reluctant smile.

"So tomorrow is my eighteenth birthday," I said. "I don't know if birthdays were ever a big thing for you growing up but they were a big deal to my parents. It always kind of annoyed me because I was an only child and I was/am an ungrateful monster. But when I realized that my birthday was coming up I wanted to do something special with someone I really cared about.

"I wanted to start this part of my life with a birthday that would mean something, that would herald this new chapter. I do remember our conversation but maybe it's just because I'm a thick idiot but I didn't get the severity of your aversion. I wasn't trying to hurt you, I swear. I swear on the golden moon or on my soul or on whatever you'd like. I don't know if you know but every summer there is a festival called," but she interrupted me.

109

Her face was pained as she said "The Starry Ocean Festival. Aye, I know it. You couldn't have picked a worse festival in a worse place at a worse time." Her words were rough but her tone was kinder as she went. Her tone was the loving exasperation of an old sister to her stupid, well-meaning idiot of a little brother. My relief came out in a hug and she exhaled the ghost of a laugh.

"I don't know how you manage to be *so* stupid," she said and my soul laughed so loud he startled me.

"I know, right!" my soul said.

"So I take it you don't want to go," I said with an impish grin as I rose to get the makings for a fire. Since we weren't going south we might as well stop for a snack and to regroup.

I didn't look over but her growl was answer enough and I chuckled. We ate bread and jerky with our hot tea and Brigitte spoke.

"The last time I saw the Starry Ocean Festival was when I was eleven. It was the day I ran away. My father loved the festival. He loved everything to do with the ocean. He used to joke that he had saltwater instead of blood running through his veins. No sea was too rough and no weather was too foreboding to keep him from his love of the waves.

"He died when I was ten. He just... didn't come back. The other fishing boat said that the waves just swallowed him, they covered him like a turning page on a book. The South Coast took everything from me that day. I haven't felt alive since. I don't think."

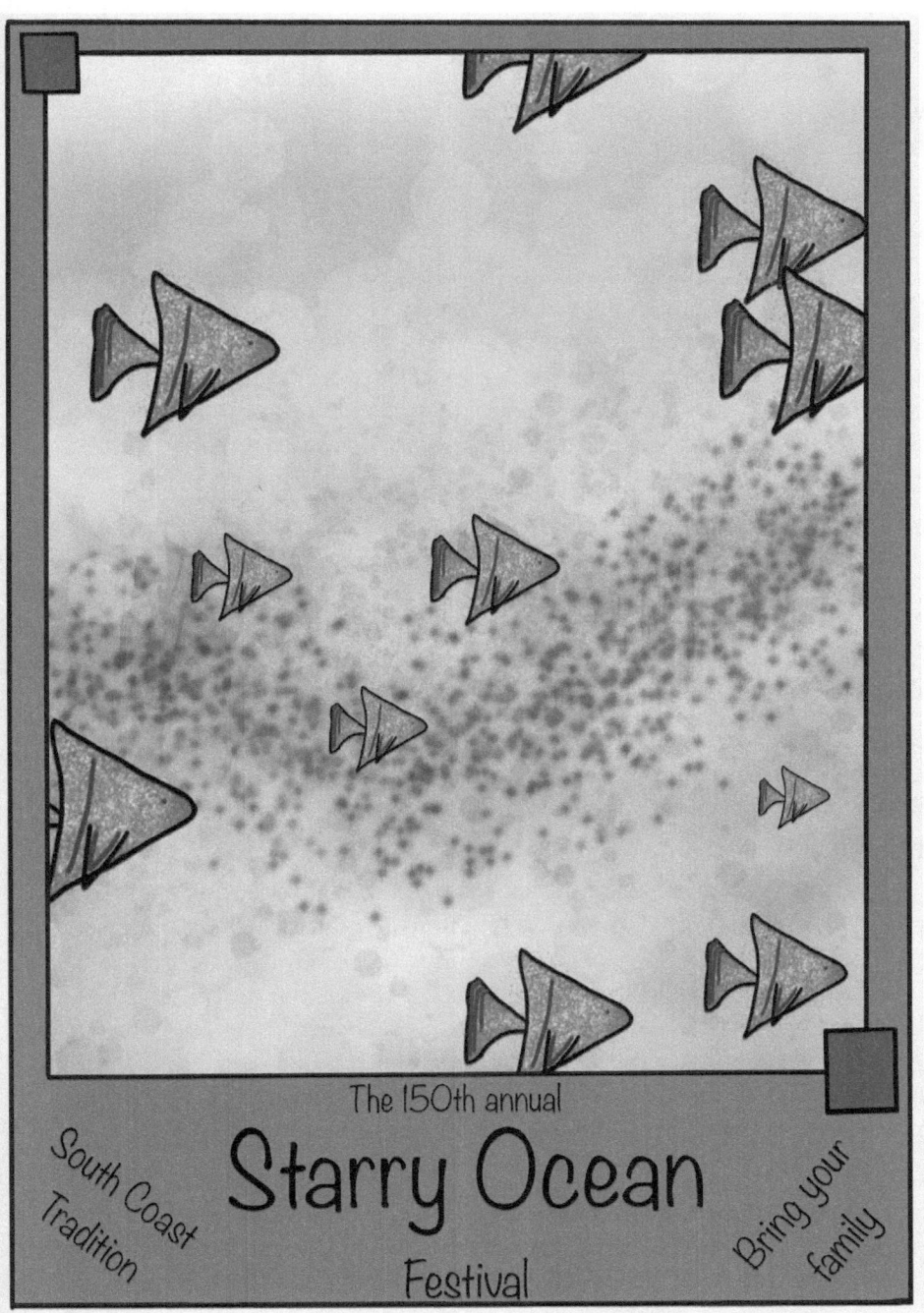

The 150th annual

Starry Ocean

South Coast Tradition

Festival

Bring your family

We waited in silence a moment as we both stared into the flames.

"What about your mother?" I asked. I should have just left it but what makes a tiny eleven-year-old Brigitte run away. It was breaking my heart and I didn't even have one. I looked over to my soul and saw what I was feeling amplified by a hundred and plastered all over his face.

Brigitte spat.

"My 'mother,'" she said and I could hear the quotations around the word, "didn't mourn my father a day. He was a good man. He was a simple, honest man. She'd always despised him for it. He wasn't reaching or ambitious. He loved only us and the ocean. I don't know if she just couldn't bear to be alone or if she finally just didn't have to be discreet but there were always men in the house after that. Bad men.

"Sometimes they hurt her, sometimes they wandered to other rooms of the house and she didn't stop them. She let them. What kind of a mother, what kind of a human lets that happen to a child? My grandmother found out what was happening and she packed me a bag with all the money she could find and sent me on my way… on the festival night. She was sick or she would have gone with me herself but she saved me.

"After that I went north. Always north. As far as I could travel but I always ended up circling the capital like a leaf caught in a drain. Becoming a princess saved me again. Meeting you saved me again. I love you, little brother."

I was speechless and furious. I wanted to scream and yell and kill everyone who had ever hurt her. The intensity of my feelings surprised me. I wished I could go back in time and protect her. My soul was crying. It was a horrible story. So much worse than the pitiful one I'd lived that I told myself was the worst thing that could ever happen to a person. I was sick with myself. Brigitte had lived a nightmare and she could still laugh. She could still smile. I never would have guessed if she hadn't have told me. She'd trusted me and I didn't know how to respond.

I should have told her my story. It was the perfect time. Even though my story was nothing compared with hers, it was the time to come clean and tell her my secrets. But something stayed my tongue.

Fear? It wasn't that I didn't trust Brigitte. I did. I loved her and only her really. Maybe I worried that knowing about Earth would put her in danger. Maybe I worried that she'd think different of me if she knew I was from another planet. I don't know why but when the moment came, when she lifted her eyes from the fire to meet mine, I said "I love you, too." It wasn't the wrong thing to say but it just wasn't the right thing.

I wanted to say more and what came out surprised all three of us. "I swear to you that no one will ever hurt you like that again." I felt the fire that had been rising in my blood from the moment I heard how she'd been used rise up to the surface. I was sure they could see it in my eyes. The need to protect her was heavy and righteous in my chest.

She wasn't my sister but she was. I never wanted to see her hurt again, from me or from anyone. She didn't say anything but she smiled and we watched the fire in companionable silence. The moment to tell her my truth was gone. My soul met my eyes and I couldn't read what he was thinking. Maybe he was relived. Maybe he was disappointed that I was such a coward. How different things might have been if she'd known.

The Seven of Us

1

Felix

I told you about how I met Felix and I'm sure you'd like to hear a pleasant story about how after we became brothers I finally understood him and the two of us worked together to teach him how to be kind.

HA HA. No. I almost laughed there at the thought. Felix didn't want much to do with us. He rarely left our Mother's side and since I tried to rarely be at her side we thankfully existed mostly on separate planes. The story about Felix that most sticks out in my brain is the last one but that really has too many spoilers so you'll have to wait for that one. Trust me you don't want to read it now. Things are better right now in the story. Let's just bask in that until I ruin it, alright?

Felix

2

Gabriel

I already told you about how Gabriel joined Brigitte and I on our first adventure. Gabriel was kind enough but he was just so boring. I wondered what his appeal had been for our mother. Because to be honest all the rest of us were so obviously broken and damaged that Gabriel seemed like he didn't fit. But he does. There is no misplaced puzzle piece in our family. We each fit like destiny shaped us for just such a purpose. Gabriel was an orphan raised by the mayor of his town, remember? And he became on orphan because he watched his parents starve as they gave him all the food. So really did he stand a chance at being a normal guy? Probably not.

He'd never let me to use his personal library. It consisted of eight floor-to-ceiling bookcases. I tried to sneak in a dozen times. Brigitte made it in once but she said that the books were boring with no pictures. She wasn't a big reader and she didn't know what I was looking for which was any mention of Earth or any another world that might give me clues on how to go home.

Each time I tried to make it into Gabriel's room he was there in moments. I'd thought that having my soul as a spy meant that I knew what was going on but Gabriel had the palace rigged. He was so clever.

He used his knowledge to charm or blackmail the guards into doing his bidding and report when little brothers tried to sneak into libraries. He wielded information like a sword against anyone that disagreed with him or anyone that wanted to hurt the family, including family members.

Gabriel loved his stupid books and it made me remember the story he'd told about his childhood. About the famine and the mayor and the library set on fire. And I have a strong feeling that the fire wasn't an accident and that it also wasn't an accident that the mayor was home when it happened. Yeah, Gabriel is one of us, all right.

Gabriel

3

Riley

I knew I *would* kill Riley before I exactly knew *why*. He's a villain like Felix and like myself, I suppose. But he's a flavor of villain even I have trouble tolerating. But let me tell you his backstory, I have a feeling you'll come around to my side of things by the end. I know a lot of his backstory because Riley at one point tried to seduce Brigitte, after she was already his sister. Yup. That's the kind of man he is. And he thought that bragging of his past would endear her to him.

Thankfully, I came quickly into the picture and he got the message that our sister was off limits, which was not a sentence I ever thought I would write. But some people are (enter expletive of your choice). I learned the rest of his story from town gossip. The castle was not far enough away from Riley's past that his reputation didn't follow him like a hound.

Riley was born in the town of Brockton. It's due west of the castle and one of the biggest towns before the West Plains. I've only been there a couple times and once I knew Riley I could pinpoint why I'd never cared for the town. It was exactly the kind of place that produces 'Rileys'.

The town was divided nearly perfectly into wealthy nobles and the poor people who lived as little better than slaves to work their mines, fields, and shops. Nowhere else in Morland is like this. I don't know why I'm defending Morland by emphasizing this point but Morland's sins do not include slavery. Well, except Brockton.

Riley lived on the wealthy side of town. He was an only child to two parents who ran a successful winery. They were extremely wealthy. They had the kind of money that made every trouble disappear, well not every trouble.

His parents died from sickness when he was seventeen and he inherited everything. He impregnated, beat, and then fired every female servant in his household. He gambled at a breakneck speed with what he was assumed was a limitless reservoir and it could have been. But the problem with his plan of "doing whatever the hell he wanted whenever the hell he wanted" was that the poor side of town, which had been quietly suffering in their bondage, found a solid figure to hate and rebel against in Riley. His treatment of their daughters, his wild temper, and spend-thrift attitude gave the servants courage.

Riley

They burned down the winery and the vineyards. They ransacked the house and stole every family heirloom and piece of furniture that wasn't nailed down. Ignorant, Riley woke up that morning at the bar where he'd gambled, drank, and caroused all night and made his lazy way home.

I smile to imagine his face when his home first came into view. And I wonder how long it took for him to ascertain the true horror of his situation. He had nothing but the ale-stained clothes on his back. He hadn't even won the previous night so all he had was debts to his name. Ahh, sometimes we get just what we deserve. And when it's not me I love to watch. Riley fled and headed to the biggest city in Morland. He thought no one would find him in the city surrounding the castle.

He found work as an assistant to the Hound Master. In Riley's old life he had done a lot of hunting and it was easy to hunt the castle's game. It was not easy to follow orders. When Riley got beaten by his master for his attitude or his laziness, he'd unleashed triple what he'd received on the first dog that came into view or the first foolish girl who was ensnared by Riley's handsome face. Because make no mistake he was a handsome man. His brown hair was thick and somehow always clean. He exercised and spoke well. The women of Morland would have been much safer if Riley looked on the outside as he truly was on the inside.

Thankfully for the dogs, the tournament started soon after. He failed the first competition, wrestling, because the only time he wrestled was when he was drunk and after he got the first black eye he'd remember that he had a sword at his belt and he'd 'win' the fight by blade instead of fist.

He did not win the second competition which was scholarly based because although he'd had the resources to learn anything, he spent his time on his own pleasure.

But then came the third competition, archery. He'd hunted as a boy and had his recent experience with a bow during his days spent hunting food for the castle with the hounds. But I've come to believe that it wouldn't have mattered if he'd performed the best at the competition or not. He was probably as doomed to be a prince as I was. You'll see as I introduce you to my siblings one by one that we are each violent cruel creatures of rage, even my sweet dear Brigitte.

Milena

4

Milena

Vain. Mean. Violent. But so so beautiful. Pray to whatever you believe in that you never meet a woman like her. I don't know where she was from and I know little about her life before she became a princess. Her weight fluctuated a good bit and I think now she must have had an eating disorder. I think Milena had a good many secrets that we all didn't know.

Her bad temper and short fuse manifested like mine did in hair of a reddish hue but hers was a much softer red, leaning toward blonde than my shock of auburn. We got off on the wrong foot right away. My evident fondness of Brigitte infuriated her. She was not accustomed to being second best and with me she always would be. Milena had a mouth that was so cruel and cutting you could almost see lash marks on the servants she berated. Nothing was good enough for her, including Brigitte.

Milena assumed that she could treat her siblings the same why she treated the world but she was very wrong. One morning at breakfast, Brigitte came down late dressed like she'd spent all night at a bar with a miscreant. We'd had a lovely time. Drinking and singing and dancing.

But breakfast came early as it often does. Brigitte was wearing last night's dress with last night's spilled ale as a perfume. Milena saw her chance and attacked. She used a dozen foul words to describe Brigitte and how she was a disgrace to the title of 'princess' and how Milena was ashamed of her. She made vulgar assumptions about Brigitte's parentage. She described the type of men who would prefer Brigitte and as she was halfway through describing what they would do to her, I came behind Milena and yanked her head back with a fist full of that strawberry hair. Her chair toppled back and she was forced to scramble as I maintained my grip on her hair. There was fear in her eyes only for a moment before it was replaced with silent rage.

"You will never speak to Brigitte again. If you do, I will sneak into your room that very night and hack off every strand of your hair. I will then take the hair to a wig maker and give the wig to the most popular whore I can find. Are we clear?"

She nodded her head and I released her. After this, Brigitte and I would breakfast in one of our rooms.

5

Jermaine

Jermaine is a nomad. An actual West nomad. I was extremely curious and hoped he'd tell me all about it. He would not.

I had met a fair amount of the other nomad clans. The East with their white-haired men and pink-haired women are obviously the easiest to spot but they travel the country and aren't always easy to locate. Since they travel they are hard to peg down for taxes and the Queen viewed this as insurrection. I've hunted down more Easties than I'd have liked. No nomad does well in a prison cell.

The South nomads are dark skinned and live on the South Coast. They speak against the Queen but they have their boats to escape in when things get too hot. And the non-nomad people of the area are loyal and protect them. It's an ecosystem that is encouraging when it seems all humanity is garbage. But it's the kind of thing that gets the Queen fired up, literally. I worry when she'll just get fed up with them.

The North nomads are dark haired and live as their name would indicate in the North. And they do a good show at hiding their anger at the Queen so they avoid her wrath. They pay taxes, sometimes.

The nomads that live in the West Plains are tanned skin with dark hair. And the Plains themselves... It's almost impossible to travel since it's pretty much a desert with tall grass and endless plains. Where is the water? Where is the shelter? Jermaine would not say. Well not until he'd had a bit to drink.

West nomads, Westies, love horses. That's pretty much the only thing people know about them and Mother let him have free reign over the stables. He'd been trying to breed the kind of horses they kept on the Plains. But they didn't do well in the city. He'd managed to birth his first foals and it turned out to be twins. But when one of them died he lost it. I heard his sobbing from a ways away.

I managed to pull him from the stall and let the servants take care of the foal. Jermaine was pretty inconsolable. It was more a wail than a cry.

"I know," I said. "I'm sorry you lost one but you've still got the other one. It'll be okay."

"No, it won't be okay," he said. "The Water Seekers are always born as twins. They can only live as twins. The other one will be dead by morning tomorrow. I have failed again. My father was right. I shame my heritage and will not learn the secrets of our horses."

"Hey," I said unsure what to do with a real conversation so I steered him to the kitchen to get him a drink for fortification. "Come on, drink up. You'll feel better. You can just try again. They are just horses."

"No, it's not just horses. It's my heritage and my birthright. It is the greatest shame for foals to die. Well the second greatest shame. I left home. I left my family. My father was our chief and when he chose my brother over me as his successor I..."

Guessing where the story was going I refilled Jermaine's glass.

"I was enraged and I killed my brother and ran away. But when I was caught and brought back for trial my father was going to kill me. So I set the camp on fire. It was the dry season and the underground rivers were barely flowing. It created a distraction but the devastation it would have caused... Now my father's curse comes true. I have no affinity with our horses. I am a disgrace to the West Plains. I am nothing."

What was I supposed to say? So he was a murderer... I was starting to wonder which of us wasn't. It was more the emotions that I didn't know how to respond to. Thankfully my soul was also listening and he said "Give him a hug or something, you idiot. At least pat his shoulder."

I went with the shoulder pat. It was obvious Jermaine regretted his choices. I could see it from the earnest open expression he wore and the tears that flowed down his cheeks. I gave his shoulder one more pat for good measure.

"I'm sorry," I said setting down the bottle as I left him to his own dark memories. And I thought I had issues.

Jermaine

6
Brigitte

You already know enough about her for now. If only there wasn't more to tell... More to come later.

7
Me

The last born. The seventh. The youngest prince. They never saw me coming.

Our Mother

1

I know nothing of her past. Nothing of who she was or where she came from. I don't even know her real name. I've only ever called her "Mother" or "the Queen". I wonder if there is anyone living on Morland who knows her name? I do know a bit of her plan, what I was able to gather anyway.

So she comes into power seventy years ago and seizes the country. She starts stealing people with magic and then the masses make a half-ass rebellion and she destroys them. Then she takes *everyone* with magic. For what? You are about to find out.

Then the young men of the country are pressured to join her army and they comply. Then she rules quietly for a long time. Until she decides for whatever reason to start the tournament and she holds the first of seven competitions. And then there was Felix and then the rest of us.

But why, right? I mean if she wanted to make seven strange bastard children why wait seventy years? I think that is because she had to. She *had* to wait that long. I don't know why though. I've never talked my theory out with anyone.

Garrison didn't care and I didn't care at first either. Brigitte saw our mother as some kind of savior or at least a benefactress. And Jol? Yeah it's kind of fun to imagine us having a campfire talk about why the Queen does what she does. And my soul? We just always had more pressing problems than speculating Mother's backstory. So, of course, now that I'm alone with just my thoughts I can't help but wonder.

2

The morning after I became prince, a servant was at my door with an invitation to afternoon tea with the Queen. I have never been to an afternoon tea before or since. I wasn't nervous exactly. Who could be nervous for a tea party in garden? But I didn't know anything about the Queen and despite the discussion with Brigitte the night before I wasn't convinced that becoming a prince *wasn't* a terrible thing.

When I left my room to find the garden, a silent servant was there to escort me. The garden was a kind of boxed area of greenery. One side was walled by the kitchens, two sides by the large dining room area, and one side to the perimeter wall that encircled the whole castle. The Queen was sitting with her back to me as she faced the simple garden only adorned with a gazebo in the center. She turned to face me before I said anything.

"Derek," she said with a small smile, "welcome." She nodded her head to indicate I was to sit across from her.

"How did you sleep last night?" she asked as she poured me a cup of tea. Being so close to her I was stunned by how beautiful she was and it took me a moment to answer. Her long black hair and pale skin were at odds with her deep red dress. She was ageless. Thirty? Forty? Definitely not more than seventy which was her true age. Her eyes were black and sharp. She wouldn't miss much.

"I slept fine, your Majesty."

"Oh no. It's 'Mother' now, my son. This is your new home and your new life."

"About that..." I said. "I'm not sure this is for me. I could just stay a solider. I was pretty good at it and I wasn't even supposed to be at the castle yesterday. I was just..."

"Enough," she interrupted her eyes flashing and her fingers sparking. I leaned back. I'd forgotten for a minute that she wasn't just a Queen but a fire Queen who'd struck some kind of deal with the Darkness. She could destroy me if she wanted to. Her words were biting when she spoke again but she smiled wide.

"I do not make mistakes, boy. You are my son now and forever. You are a prince. This is your home. You are safe now." Everything she was saying sounds nice but imagine a giant snake saying those things to you while it hugged you tighter and tighter. *This is your home. You are safe now.* Still repeating as it swallowed you whole. *You are safe now.* That's how she sounded and that's how it felt.

The room didn't look any different but there was a chill and the Darkness, which though always there like an ill breeze or something wrong in the air, was stronger now more like a blasting wind forcing me to plant my feet and bend to keep from toppling. She was in control of the Darkness somehow. I didn't feel the pressure abate until I nodded.

"This will be a good life. You'll see, my dear, " she took a sip of her tea and when her eyes went to my cup I copied her. "You have wealth, resources, your siblings... You'll be very happy here. I am sure."

The Queen raised her hand and I heard a servant girl rush over. She was carrying a heavy tray full of cakes and treats. I don't know if the girl was nervous or just clumsy but she tripped and the tray clattered and crashed sending the food everywhere.

"Idiot!" the Queen roared. Her mood swings were giving me whiplash. She sure had a quick temper. We had more in common than I was comfortable admitting. It seemed I would fit right into the family.

The girl hurried to clean the mess but she was shaking pretty bad. I instinctually moved to help her but the Queen said "Stay." I looked at her and the fire that had enveloped her whole hand made me slowly take my seat. The Queen smiled at my obedience and flicked her wrist at the girl, encasing her body in flames.

Without thinking I jumped up and rushed to the girl but a fire ball in the middle of my back sent me to my knees. I gasped at the intense pain, crying out. I looked to the girl still in flames but she was silent. The Queen noticed too.

"Interesting," she said snapping her fingers as the flame disappeared from the girl. She wasn't burned. Instead she just seemed wet. I sighed. The girl had magic, some kind of water magic. This wasn't going to end well.

"Guards," the Queen said and four men came from the hallway to drag the girl to a prison cell. I almost smiled for a second as I realized that this was my chance to find out what she did with them, all the people she took with magic. I must have actually smiled because the Queen beamed as she walked over to me.

"I'm sorry if that stings but when I say 'stay' you stay. I am your mother but also your queen. I will be obeyed."

"Yes, Mother," I said bowing my head low.

"You are excused. See that your burn is treated," she patted the top of my head and left.

The burn healed but left a perfect circle of scarred skin in the center of my back. I went to check on the girl that evening. She was in a cell but fine beyond that. She was the only one there. Where was everyone else with magic?

I kept checking on the girl but she just stayed in the cell. She was fed and given basic necessities. It just didn't add up. I found the truth on accident a month later. It was a bright night with a full moon. Brigitte and I had gone drinking and were making our drunken way back home to the castle. I'd dropped B off at her rooms and I passed the garden on the way to mine.

The Queen stood in the middle of the small space under the gazebo with only the light of a floating fireball to light the garden. The servant girl sat bound and gagged at the Queen's feet. Water pooled around her as the girl tried to fight back. But she had no real control of her magic.

I stood watching from the shadows transfixed in horror imagining only one after for the girl. She struggled as the Queen moved closer but fire was not to be her fate. The Queen grabbed a fist-full of the girl's hair with her non-fire hand. The girl's head jerked back and in one swift motion the fire went out and the sound of gurgling filled the space.

I knew that sound. I didn't need light to know that the Queen had slit her throat. There was a thud as the girl slumped forward. I turned to leave sickened but I stopped, frozen. A tremor shook the garden. The Darkness poured into the space drowning out the traces of moonlight. I thought I saw shapes in the black but maybe it was my eyes playing tricks with me. I left as quietly as I could and proceeded to not sleep a wink.

That murdering woman was my mother now.

3

She was a solitary creature, our mother. She had no friends, no lover. Just her soldiers, the seven of us, and Jol. She had no hobbies but world domination and to be fair she was so good at it she didn't need to crochet to fill the time. One thing she did love was the sound of her own voice.

Whenever she summoned me or all of us. She spent most of the time talking. Talking about our glorious future. But she also talked to herself. My soul is a terrible snoop, comes with being invisible to most everyone and stuck with only me as a companion. The Queen would talk to us about our 'glorious futures' but that was not what she said to herself.

"She's craaaaazzzzzy," my soul said one night after waking me up with several loud verses of "The Maiden Who Married Your Cousin", an annoying, repetitive pub song that he had memorized and liked to recite at length and at great volume. He didn't have many weapons he could use against me nor I him but he/we have a terrible singing voice.

"What?" I said sitting up and taking a swing at my soul. I knew that I couldn't punch him but I wanted him to know that I would if I could.

"Mother. She's bonkers. I know we've had our concerns but we wanted to hold off judgement since we've only been in the castle for a month but we might should keep looking for the way home."

That got my attention. I hadn't been looking for the portal as much. I'd been unofficially exiled to the north for a while after I'd killed the general's son. And then I'd become prince and Brigitte had me running around having fun. I'd almost forgotten. It seemed impossible. I'd almost forgotten that Morland was not my home.

"I know we should keep looking," I said sitting up and rubbing my eyes. "It's just been crazy around here."

"Yup. Yup. Yup," my soul said. "Wanna know why it's crazy? Cause the show is being run by Mrs. Momma Crazy Pants."

"What are you talking about?" I said. "Just get to your point. It's really early or late. I can't tell which but I'm tired."

"She talks to herself. She's been talking to herself for *hours*," he said drawing out the last word. "And not just like 'Oh I forgot to water the plant. Note to self.' No, you don't get it, Derek. It's like she's two people or like she's not alone. She talked about all of you. Your strengths and weaknesses and how she expected you to change when 'it' happens. Something is coming, Derek. She's planning something. She said, and I quote, 'When Derek has been changed, Morland will be reborn into a new age of Darkness. We'll be able to change the very foundation of the world.' End quote. She also has these creatures, have you seen them?"

"No," I said getting dressed. I was never going to get back to sleep after this conversation. "What kind of creatures? What do they look like?"

"Like smoke made out of velociraptor claws."

"Oh good. It seemed for a minute that Morland was getting better or at least treating us better. I thought I saw something in the Darkness when she killed that servant girl. Nice to know I wasn't imagining it. But I wonder if the smoke creatures are only in the spirit realm. I've never seen them before or since. You've got company it would seem."

"Yeah. Awesome," he said rolling his eyes. "Thank goodness I've got this at least." He patted the sword at his waist. One of the only items he was able to touch, that and his clothes. He'd threatened to go nude forever but worried that if he took his clothes off he wouldn't be able to touch them again. It was too high a cost to annoy even me.

"Okay, so we resume the search for the tree," I said. "It looks like our time as prince has a clock on it. I hope the Queen doesn't have plans to do anything to Brigitte."

My soul met my eyes and I sighed.

"It's been a while since we've said this but…"

"Morland is the worst," we said in unison.

Full Moons

1

It took me as long as it did to notice that my siblings were different because I was gone so much and the little changes barely caught my notice. Dark eyes. Aggression. Neither of those things on their own really meant anything in our motley crew.

I didn't notice the changes in Felix because his badness level felt maxed out and his eyes were already a dark color. But when Gabriel got into a fight with a woman in the marketplace barely stopping before he beat her to death, I made myself open my eyes. Something was happening. Maybe *it* was happening.

I barely had time to investigate when whatever it was happened to Riley. I bumped into him in the hallway and he stabbed me in the shoulder. Out of the blue, just stabbed me. It wasn't deep but it stung. I got a very good look at his eyes and they were black. All of it was black. And they gleamed like a snake's. He walked by just letting my blood drip from the dagger onto the floor. His shiny new medallion caught my eye as he passed. It had a moon and three stars on it. I let him leave unchallenged and brought my concerns to Brigitte.

"Something strange is happening around here," I told her that night while we had dinner in her rooms.

"Like what?" she asked passing a tray to me.

"Like half of our siblings have gone insane. I mean you saw what Riley did to me," I said showing her my bandaged shoulder. "And what about Gabriel?" I asked her.

"Yes. That was very strange. Have you seen their eyes?" she asked me.

"Yes! They are black and glossy. After I saw Riley, I looked at Felix and Gabriel. Theirs are black too. I don't like it, B. Just keep an eye out, okay?"

"We could keep four eyes out if you were home more. I had to nearly gut Philip, the night guard, for getting too frisky with me. He wouldn't take no for an answer. I asked if he'd take my dagger for an answer. He said he'd try his luck another time. What good is a sword-fighting champion brother if he can't even defend his sister's honor?"

"Oh my dear. You can take care of yourself. No one would dare mess with you twice," I said kissing her forehead. She huffed but accepted the compliment.

I started watching Milena like a hawk waiting for whatever it was to happen to her. It had been going in order and she was next. It happened in the middle of the month, the day after the full moon. One day she was preening and ordering and the next she was like a panther set loose in the castle. I could tell it had happened just by the way she walked. Her black eyes and shiny new medallion, hers with a crescent moon and four stars, were only confirmation. Whatever the medallions were, I felt certain mine would have seven stars on it.

Seven
Medallions

Brigitte warned Jermaine that something might happen to him at the next full moon. He went straight to Mother. She then called Jermaine, Brigitte and I in for an audience.

"Jermaine tells me that you two have concerns about your siblings?"

I barely contained my glare at Jermaine.

"They have been acting strange. Their eyes are black and they are not the same people they were. We want to know what's happening," I said.

"And you will," she said smiling. I hated it when she smiled. She smiled before she whipped a servant boy. She smiled before she set a cat on fire. She smiled whenever she spoke to me. "It is a gift. You'll each get a chance."

"I don't want it," I told her. Brigitte glanced at me shocked at my outburst.

"You don't even know what it is," the Queen said.

"What is it?"

Her eyes narrowed. "You aren't ready to know yet. Jermaine stay. I'll see you two when it's your turn. Stay out of trouble. Oh Derek, I'm sorry for Riley. He won't hurt you again. None of your siblings will," she said as the door closed in our face.

"What are we going to do?" Brigitte asked me.

"We are going to watch what happens to Jermaine next month."

And we did watch.

On the night of the full moon, Jermaine went alone into the garden. He stood under the gazebo and slashed his arm with a knife. It was so unexpected and we might have commented on it but then before we could draw a breath Jermaine was swallowed up by the Darkness.

It congealed into a dark mass around him seeming to erase him from existence. But even though we couldn't see him, we could hear him. His screams cut through my skin and seemed to suck all the air out of my lungs. Brigitte nearly squeezed my fingers off as we stared silently in horror. After a moment it all stopped. The Darkness dissipated and Jermaine walked out of the garden like nothing had happened. His eyes were black.

"Oh Goodness, I'm next," Brigitte whispered long after Jermaine had gone. She knelt down and prayed soft spoken prayers into the ground. I didn't have the heart to tell her that there was no one to listen.

"We'll find a way, B. Don't worry. I'll always protect you," I said.

That night I went to find Jol. I hoped he had answers. This will be the worst mistake of my entire life. If I live to be a hundred, this will still be the worst mistake.

Jol was no help as usual. I don't know what I'd expected. I had been gone for two days and I was anxious being away from Brigitte. She was not going to leave my side until we figured it out. It took me half a day to find her. She was usually waiting for me in the stables. She somehow always knew when I would come home. But she wasn't there. She wasn't in her room and she wasn't in my room. I found her in the dungeon beneath the castle watching a man vomit.

"Hey sis, have you really been this bored since I've been gone?" I asked pulling her into a hug. She flinched away from my touch and continued watching the man.

"Who is..." I started to ask until I realized who it was in the cell. It was Philip, the guard, and he was vomiting blood.

"He wouldn't listen. My dagger didn't stop him," she said without looking at me. "He held me down and raped me. He was bleeding from his wounds but he didn't stop. Then we were both bleeding. Do you see how tall he is? I wasn't strong enough to push him off."

I felt like I might join him in vomiting. I had left Brigitte and the worst thing that could have ever happened to her had happened. Her mom's suitors often wandered to Brigitte's room. She ran away at eleven and never took a lover. To have a man force himself on her... I tentatively reached for her. I knew it was selfish but if I could comfort her, I would be able to assuage my own guilt.

"Don't touch me!" she yelled and it echoed on the walls, replaying over and over. "Where were you? Where were you, Derek? You left me and he.... You left me and he hurt me. You promised you would always protect me. You promised. You said that would never happen again. You said that I could count of you," she said brokenly turning back to look at cell. "When I told Mother, she told me I could have him. The water has been poisoned. It makes him terribly thirsty and he can't stop drinking it. It's nearing the end. He'll be dead in the morning."

I left her to watch the man she was murdering die. I threw up in the hallway. The days until the full moon haunted me like a chiming clock. She wouldn't speak to me and I knew she was going to do it. Whatever it was. Whatever the Queen had done to our siblings, Brigitte was going to do it to herself.

2

During the month as I waited for *it* to come for Brigitte, my soul and I had the same conversation over and over just using different words as we tried to come at it from different angles.

"Okay. The facts," I said sitting across from him on the floor.

"The facts," my soul said.

Just settling into our familiar problem solving seats made me calmer. My soul has a way of showing me the truth of a situation and not just the horror in it. It suddenly becomes easier to bear. Easier to face. When he's not with me... It can be unbearable. But together, we can't be stopped.

"Okay, so during the full moon the Queen has made our siblings go into the garden at night and the Darkness attacks them? Changes them?" I said.

"Yeah. It's weird," he said nodding and shrugging. "So Fact #1: It's triggered by the full moon. And that leads into Fact #2: It has happened to each of us one at a time and in order."

"That seems important," I said. "It's not random. It's a calculated event that is happening on purpose. But what is it?"

"How has Jermaine seemed to you?"

It took me minute to find the words. Not that I could have a secret from my soul but all I could think about was that Brigitte was next. And I had to look around a minute for the mental file about anyone else but her.

"He's... a monster," I said. There was no other way to say it. Before the full moon Jermaine had been quiet, self-contained. Yes, he'd murdered his brother but as long as I'd known him I'd never seen that side of him. And now...

"He's loud, violent, cruel. He killed half the horses in the stable... for fun. He drinks like a fish, like he's starving for it, like he's gonna die if he's not drunk. He's like an uncontrollable ball of rage."

"So the Darkness turned him into something else?"

I bit my cheek. "No. It's like... It's like the Darkness set him loose. Like he'd been keeping all that locked away and now he has no filters and no boundaries. I'd hate to see what it would let free inside of me... or Brigitte."

"There has got to be a way to stop it!" my soul said pounding his fist on his knees. He flinched. He couldn't interact with the world but he could touch anything on his person like his clothes, shoes, hair, or sword. It was curious that when we'd crossed over he'd been the one given a sword. He practiced when I practiced and I'm sure he was pretty good. Although he could never spar with anyone. He gripped the hilt of his sword and I knew he wished this was something he could fight. But we were both helpless in this.

"How do we save her?" he asked.

"I don't know. We'll just have to keep an eye on her. We'll stop her before the time comes. We just have to hope, no we *have* to make an opening to talk to her again. Make her listen."

The month was up and she was walking out into the dark garden. It was now or never. Our last chance to save her. She must have known I would follow her that night. I revealed my presence when the gazebo was finally in sight. I couldn't let her go another step.

It's coming...

Killing My Sister

1

"B!" I called out, running to catch up with her. "Stop. Don't go in there." The gazebo looming behind her shone in the moonlight.

"Brother Derek, you came. Welcome," she said smiling but her tone chilled me. She was mad. The lethal kind. A dark fury roiled beneath her surface. Then suddenly her smile was gone. "How nice that you stayed in town long enough. Thank you for putting your very important secret businesses on hold." She took another step away from me.

"Stop," I said again as I caught up with her. "Going in there will turn you into a monster. Brigitte, please talk to me. You've seen our siblings! Something bad is happening and it is related to the full moons. You don't know what will happen to you."

"Yes. I know exactly what will happen to me. I'm trading in my soul for power. And then I will join our siblings. I will be the strongest of us all. No one will be able to hurt me when I'm done."

As she turned away from me I saw the fading bruises on her arms and the reminder of how I had failed her fell over me like a bucket of ice water.

"I'm so sorry. I will never let anything happen to you again. I'm sorry. How many times do I have to say it? Let's go. Just the two of us. We'll leave Mother and our siblings. We'll leave the kingdom. Come with me." I was getting desperate. I would do anything to keep her from going through those arches.

Her eyes were brimstone and fire.

"I don't need your protection anymore!" she spat as she ran for the opening. I tackled her and we rolled. "I will be strong!" she howled as she pulls out a dagger. She slashed my right side without hesitation. I pulled back in shock and it was enough for her to dive inside the archway. She slashed her right wrist with the same dagger and then threw it at my feet. I dragged myself over but it was too late.

A black cloud of Darkness filled the pavilion and it felt like a solid wall against my pounding fists. Her screams made me frantic and I slashed at the Darkness wall with her dagger trying to free her. Nothing was working and in my hopelessness I prayed that if there was anything good in the world that it would spare my sister, that it would protect her from her choices.

The Darkness slowly dissipated and Brigitte walked out. She ignored me and would have passed me by but I grabbed her hand.

"B, what have you done?" I said. That hadn't been what I planned on saying but her face was so altered it just burst out. Her eyes were completely black. The whole thing. The soft gold was gone and all I could see was a fathomless black.

"I am not to harm you, last born. But get out of my way," she said pushing past.

"Oh, your eyes," I said in a broken voice. "No! No. Brigitte. Wait, wait it's not too late." I pleaded after her, despair filling me. "There must be something we can do. We can fix this."

"There is nothing to *fix,*" she said the word slowly. Staring at me. "I wanted this. This is my choice. I will present myself to my queen as ordered and then I will go to the South Coast and burn it and everyone in it to the ground."

"No, you don't mean that," I said. "It's just the Darkness speaking. I know a lot of bad things happened there but think of all the innocent people. All the children. And your grandmother might still be alive."

"*All will burn.* I will finally have a fresh start. The past will hold no claim on me when all is ash."

She was so serious and she was scaring the crap out of me. I threw all my weight to take her down. I had to knock some sense into her. Straddling her, I yelled, "This isn't you! This is the Darkness! I'm not letting you go until you see reason."

"This is not the Darkness. I have always wanted this," she said snaking her hand up to rest on my side. "Only now I have the strength," she said pressing her hand to the knife wound she had given me only minutes ago. "Only now I'm not afraid!" she said punching her fist into the wound.

I rolled over in pain watching as Brigitte ran out through the kitchen. Two thoughts filled my mind as blood poured out my side. She was going to burn them all to ash. And she had disobeyed two orders.

I had to stop her but I couldn't think over the keening wail in my mind. The despair was fighting to take control but I shoved down the mourning. It wasn't time yet. There still had to be some time.

I tied my cloak around my wound, grabbed a horse, and went to my only ally in the whole world.

"I've been researching since we spoke last month..." He was having trouble telling me whatever it was.

"Just spit it out. There isn't time for this."

"Derek, I don't know if you ever realized that I'm not a good man. In all this world how many mages have you met? That's right, only two. The Queen and myself. We share the same fire affinity. She felt that it gave us a kinship and since I cannot harm her with her own power, I was allowed to live... for a price. I became the masked soldier stealing children from their homes and fathers from their sons. When you do what I've done, a certain amount of Darkness takes place in your soul.

"I took my life in exchange for so many many people. She killed them all. The people I stole. She slit their throats in the garden. Always over the same spot." Jol stepped toward me and I realized I had been walking backwards. Jol had known and he'd done nothing. He could have warned me. He could have told me when I'd come last month.

I'd seen the Queen kill someone in the garden when I first became a prince. Only then I'd had no idea what was going on. Now I knew and it was too late. It had been a sacrifice to the Darkness. That spot, the red stained spot was under the gazebo in the garden. It was the place where... I couldn't finish the thought and Jol just kept talking.

"But when I met you, you gave me a purpose again," he continued. "I decided I wanted to try and be a better man. I haven't killed anyone since that day. Not that it mattered. Not that not killing atones for anything in my soul. I only confess all this to tell you to let you know that I know a little something about the Darkness. And what your Mother is doing is flooding her children with it. It fills all of them. It fills their souls. It makes them obedient to her and gives each party unbelievable powers. Brigitte's soul is gone, Derek. She is gone."

"No, there has to be a way to fix it," I said shaking my head. "I don't accept this. I can't. I mean, she disobeyed an order from the Queen. She hurt me and she wasn't heading to the Queen like she said she was supposed to. She left through the kitchens. She was leaving the castle. She was heading south. There is still hope. We'll figure something out."

"Yes, that is peculiar but in disobeying, she caused pain and suffering," he said trying to reason with me. "Had she tried to disobey to do an act of goodness... I'd have more hope. She is bound to the

Darkness and the Darkness brings out the worst in a person, their most selfish, cruel, hateful tendencies. So there will be some flexibility if the actions are within those parameters. And the bond is new, maybe it takes time to settle. But, Derek, she cannot be *un*bound. It's not so much of a binding. It's more of an exchange. She has given up herself to make room for power. It's not that the Darkness is in control. It's that the old Brigitte isn't even in there to fight."

I remember the horror washing over me. I can still taste it even now. "What do I do then?" I said brokenly sliding to the floor as tears fell without thought. I didn't care that I was a solider, that I was a grown man now. I pounded the ground with my fists.

"It's all my fault!" I yelled. "I promised to always protect her. I was gone. And she got... He... Something happened and it broke her. And now my sister is gone. Oh God! What have I done? It's all my fault. It's all my fault. Oh God!" I cried clutching my bleeding wound, yelling with rage.

"Let's work on the things we can fix first," Jol said rolling me over to start cleaning my wound.

"I've got to stop her. She's going to kill everyone to ash," I said finally becoming delirious from my loss of blood. "Ash. Black eyes."

2

I wouldn't let the old man drug me. I had to be back on the road as soon as possible. He wanted me to go after her but for his own reason. We left on bad terms and I didn't know if I would ever be able to look at him the same for what he had suggested. I caught up with her the next night. She had skipped seeing Mother after all and chose vengeance. I thought I was prepared to see her. I'd already caught a glimpse of the Darkness in her but the change of twelve hours was shocking. Every smudge of humanity was gone from her. She turned her soulless black eyes on me.

"Go and await your moon, last born," she said turning away from me.

"Where are you going?" I asked

"To burn the South Coast to ash," she said without feeling.

"I can't let you do that."

Jol had told me what I should do but I didn't believe him. There had to be another option. I was going to restrain her somehow and lock her in a room until I could undo it. She was stronger now and I had trouble keeping a hold on her. We tumbled on the ground for a minute until I ended on top. My hands were at her throat, I just wanted to knock her out. She was too strong and I was too injured for an extended fight.

Suddenly before my eyes, her *eyes* changed. They became her soft gold and I heard her whisper, "Free me." In shock I let up my grip and her eyes were suddenly black again and she was fighting against it. Had that really been my sister speaking? Had I freed her for a second?

"She is never coming back," said a voice from Brigitte's lips, my hands tightened. She was finally starting to pass out and her eyes flashed gold again. "Please kill me. Release me."

I couldn't do it. How could I kill my sister? The one person I loved in the whole world. But her eyes had been filled with horror and despair and it was too much. She was surely regretting her bargain and how could I deny her last request? If she wanted to be released from the hell she was trapped in, I would do it for her. I loved her enough. I made myself watch as her eyes flickered and then went lifeless. She had mouthed thank you and then was gone.

I retched for a long while. I couldn't look at her. I felt a terrible yearning deep in myself and it felt like my insides would burst from my skin. I was shaking. I dug her grave with my hands. The dirt stuck under my nails made me feel numb. I kissed her brow as tears fell flowing and unstoppable from my eyes. I had killed the only good thing in the whole world. I think I killed myself that day.

3

I found that I couldn't leave her grave so easily. I just kept thinking about how she was all alone down there. Alone and in the dark. If I was in despair, then my soul was inconsolable. His howling grief made chills rise up my spine.

"We should go," I told him. I wanted us to go together. I couldn't imagine walking away from this grave alone.

"No no no no no," he said kneeling over the fresh dirt, resting his head on the grave.

"Come on," I said.

His eyes flashed up and they were empty and so full at the same time. Like a bottomless void of nothingness. So much nothing.

"It can't be her in there. It can't be," he said finally speaking. "Of all the people in Morland, it cannot be my sister in that grave. I can't stand it, Derek. I can't. Oh God what have we done?" He clutched his heart and just stared at me like I had an answer. I obviously did not. He was the soul. I was just the hands that killed.

"What had to be done, soul. I hate it, too. I hate this! But it is done," I said trying to be kind.

"How can you be so calm? How can you bear to leave her? I feel a black hole inside my chest that is trying to consume me. I can't breathe. I feel like I'm dying but I can't die, can I? There is no relief from this pain! I can hardly bear the weight of it here where I can see the dirt and remember her death. But if I leave this place? I can't be away from her. Do you feel one-tenth of what I feel right now? If you did you'd be trying to rip your skin off. Oh, it keeps hitting me. I forget for a moment and then I see this grave and I remember." He just closed his eyes and rested his head on her grave and wept.

"I know, soul. I know. I miss her, too. I loved her, too," I said.

He looked up at me in disgust. "I somehow envy and despise you for what you are feeling right now. If you could feel this," he said grabbing a fistful of his shirt right over his heart, "If you could feel this, it would kill you. It's killing me. I wish it was killing me. It's too much, Derek. This pain is too much. You think your pain is unbearable? I want to die," he cried. "But I can't. Or can I?"

He sat up and pulled his sword free from its scabbard.

"Hey," I said trying to grab it from him but the sword just like himself was in the spirit world, just out of my reach.

He pricked the tip of his finger with the blade and a drop of blood pooled out. I looked at my own finger and I thought I felt something, maybe. A look of relief passed over his face as he pulled the sword out and did one long cut across his left wrist.

"No!!!" I yelled still trying to touch him, to stop this new madness. I couldn't lose them both. They could not die on the same day. I was kneeling down to be in my soul's face when I felt it. I looked at my arm and saw a white line forming. I didn't feel so good.

"Please, soul! Stop. Put some pressure on the wound. Please. You are hurting me, too," I said appealing to his selflessness.

He looked up and saw that his actions were affecting my body too.

"I'm sorry," he said. He took off his cloak and began to shakily rip it into strips. He then bound his wrist and tied a knot pulling it tight with his teeth.

"Thank you," I said. "I'm sorry you hurt so much. I'm here."

We both left and never came back. And we never spoke of that again but we didn't have much time left together anyway. This evening was the beginning of the end. Thank goodness.

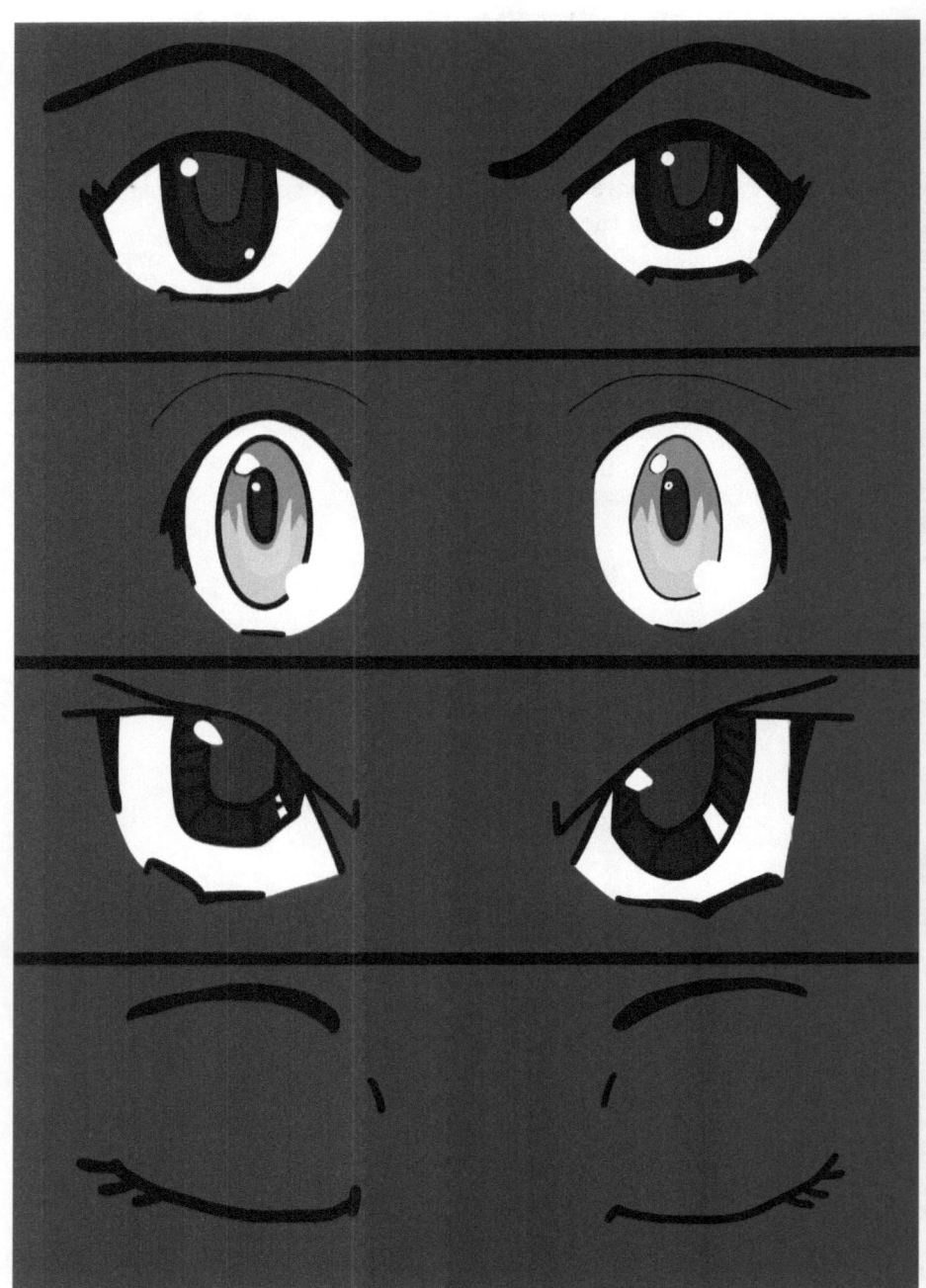

Becoming an Only Child Again

1

No one knew what I had done except Jol. I found myself at his door and screamed at him for being right. The only way to save her had been to kill her.

He opened his door and didn't yell back which was a first. He grabbed my shoulders and pulled me in. I don't remember much of that night. But I know I drank everything in his house. Everything. He told me I'd done the right thing. I told him I hated him.

I left the next morning without looking at him and headed to my room in the castle. I was deciding if I should leave the dirt caked under my nails forever when I was summoned to an audience with the Queen. I decided to change and wash. I hadn't expected all my siblings to be there. I guessed she knew what I had done and was going to kill me. I couldn't muster any fear. What a relief for it to all be over. Maybe I'd be with Brigitte again.

Gabriel spoke first. "What happened, Mother? I felt a great shift."

The others nodded around me. *A shift in what?* I wondered.

"Where is Brigitte?" Jermaine asked counting us.

"I fear that something has happened to her," the Queen said as she looked at me and I wondered what my face looked like. It must have been the appropriate response to hearing my favorite sister was missing because she continued on. "There was a disturbance in the bond that ties us all. Be careful my children. I hope it was an accident. She was supposed to come to me immediately after the full moon but... Best just be on your guard, my dears. That is all. I will alert you when I find her."

I left the room in shock. The Queen didn't know. But they'd all felt something when Brigitte died. My idea was confirmed when Riley said, "And the bitch took power with her. Don't you feel it? There is less now," he grumbled walking past without looking at me.

My soul stayed away after Brigitte. I'd see him sometimes and he always seemed like there was something he wanted to say but he didn't. Which for was the best. He couldn't have stopped me. My obsessive nature had found a new fixation: killing the woman I had called "Mother".

She had done this. *She* had broken everything. Brigitte would never have sold her soul to the Darkness if their Mother hadn't made her. She must have convinced Brigitte it was the only option, that it was the only way to be strong. That woman was going to pay for it. She was going to pay for everything she had broken in the world.

And then it struck me, the most horrible thought I would ever think. My siblings were tied together and their powers were tied to the Queen. The only way to ever stop her was to get rid of them first. What was five more really? When I'd killed the one I loved most first. It would be easy.

Riley got the slit throat he'd had coming for a long while. I caught him outside of his favorite pub as he was relieving himself. He was the perfect one to kill first because he really deserved it. His reign of terror on the young women in the capital was finally over. They should throw me a parade but I made sure no one saw me. I had a long list of kills yet to make.

Next was Jermaine. I made it look like he fell from his horse. I snapped his neck on the trail he rode every day and sent the horse running.

Milena fled. She'd been away from the castle a lot and I found her visiting a village woman and her small family. I waited till she left and stabbed her in the back before she even heard me. It didn't make sense that she was there but then again I didn't know her at all.

It got easier, taking lives. I told myself it had to be done. I told myself they weren't even really alive. I told myself I was avenging Brigitte's murder as sick as that was.

The Queen was getting restless. She loved to talk to herself and she was frantic with their deaths. My soul would sit for hours, listening to her rage and fear. He would stop in to tell me that she didn't suspect me and that she was indeed weakening. It was my resolve.

I found Felix out in the woods. I don't know what he was doing out there but he was waiting for me. I don't think he knew *who* was coming for him but he knew someone was. He laughed when he saw it was me.

"Really?" he said. "You? You are the one who has been going after us? I can't believe none of them killed you first." His eyes were hungry. I felt a ripple of fear ride up my neck. Felix with his soul made me wary and nervous. Felix without his soul was terrifying. I should have waited until he was sleeping but it was too late now. He took a step toward me but I moved easily back.

"To be fair to them," I said. "They didn't exactly see me coming."

"Do you remember when Riley stabbed your arm?" he asked moving forward and forcing me to step back again.

"Yes," I said watching him and trying to ignore the mind game he was setting up.

"After that Mother called Riley in and ordered him not to harm you again. She gave the same order to each sibling as they were made anew. But she never gave that order to me. I'm not going to kill you," he said cracking his knuckles. "But you are going to beg for it."

I won't go into the fight. I don't really want to. I don't feel any guilt about it but it had all the violence and madness of putting down a rabid mountain lion. It had to be done but even now I'm still just exhausted from it. It wasn't pretty. I barely got out with my life and it left a bad taste in my mouth. I buried him which was probably more than he deserved. His medallion with its moon and solitary star had come off in the fight. I set it on top of the mound and left.

Last was Gabriel. I only felt bad because he knew death was coming for him. I tried to be gentle. His routine never altered and poisoning his evening tea was easy enough even with four guards on alert at each door. They didn't think to test his food.

I write this down because I know it was wrong. I knew that somewhere in my mind but I still did it. I let myself imagine they would thank me but none of their eyes changed back like Brigitte's did. In truth it was just murder. They weren't being freed from anything. I feel it all now. Now that the axe doesn't hang so low over my neck. I feel each one but what's done is done. I can't change it and I probably wouldn't.

It is what it is.

2

Nope. Nope. I should erase all that and start again. It's not enough. In two ways. The first is that it probably accomplished nothing and the second is... they deserve more. No one here on Earth knew them. No one who will read this will know them but they were real and...

I don't have anything else to say.

But the Queen sure did. Her frustration and rage were terrifying. And she never thought for one single minute that one of us had done it. Did she know when it was just Gabriel and I at the end? No. But I don't know what she imagined was capable of killing one her monster children except one of us.

My soul was terrified and fascinated by her tirades. She would go into her chambers and scream and let the fire fly from her hands like torrents.

"How!" she screamed. "It isn't possible. Tell me how?"

No one answered her, of course. She was alone except for the soul she couldn't see.

She recounted each of their deaths and tried to find what tied them together. She had always assumed that no one was powerful enough to kill them or stand against her.

Then she found a nice scapegoat.

"The nomads... Of course. Who has defied me longer or bolder than them? And it all stems from the South Coast. But all is not lost. Gabriel and Derek still live. I'll keep them both guarded. No one could kill them in the castle. Each of the others was killed outside. Yes, that will keep them safe. Derek's full moon is days away when that is done all will be well. Yes, all will be well."

I fled the castle as fast as I possibly could. Gabriel's tea was on the way to his room and I was not going to be trapped here. But what now? After Gabriel was dead, what was next? Kill her? How? Hide forever? I liked the sound of that. There were a couple places that would work for now. That was the benefit of having travelled so much of Morland. I knew a couple spots where no one would find me.

But instead of running north, instead of get as far away as I could, I stopped by Jol's for one last argument. I knew how every line would go. We'd done this scene many times over the years but I had to try one last time. Because "*it* would probably never work."

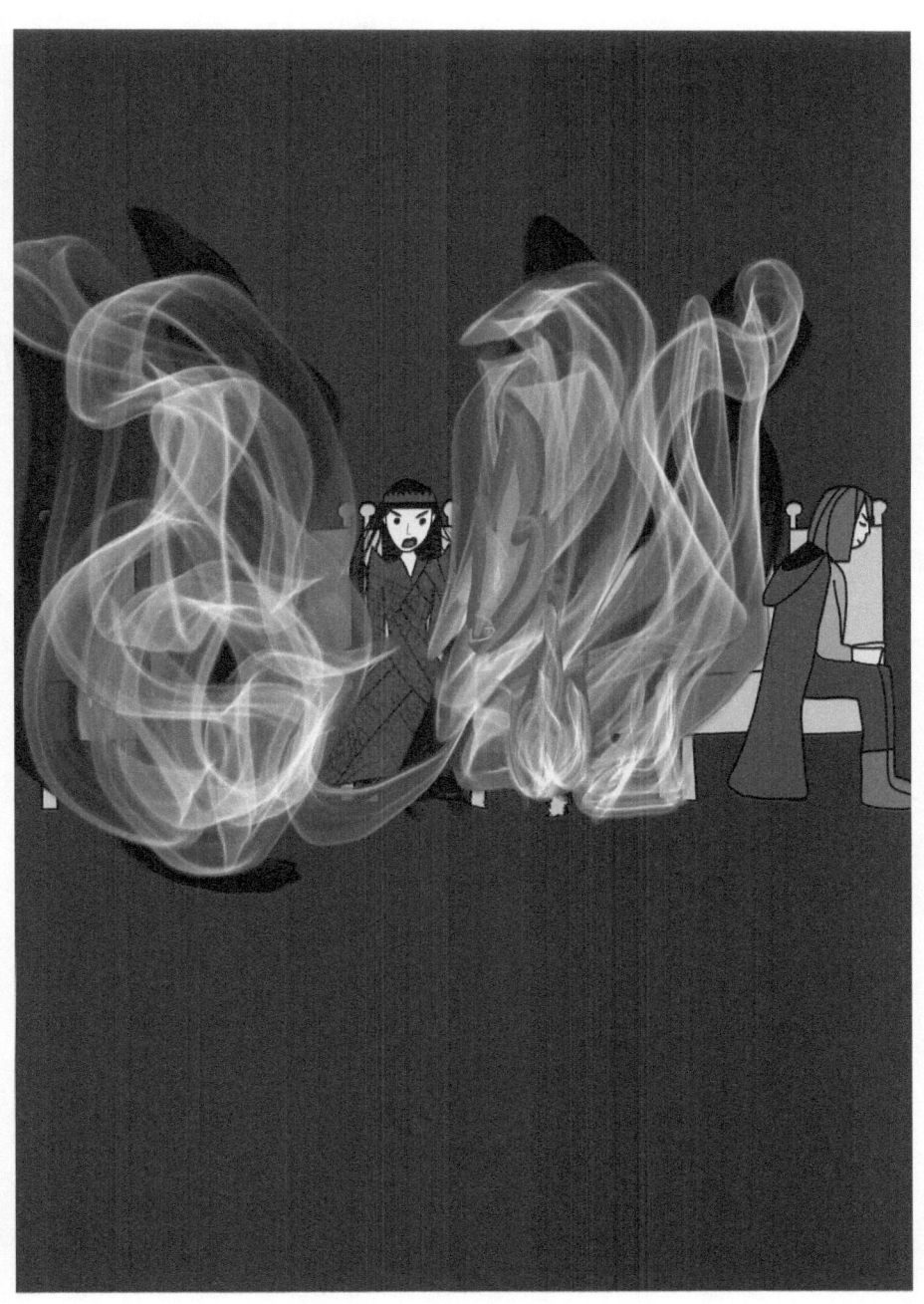

Home

1

I'd thought that becoming an only child again would be liberating. I'd imagined that the deaths of my siblings would destroy that monster of a Queen, mother of ours. But it didn't and she was now coming for me with no distractions to slow her down. I shouldn't have bothered running in the woods. First, because there was no hiding from her. The moon felt like her searchlight tagging me through the moonlight branches. And second, because if I hadn't found the way back home in the five years I'd been trapped on Morland it wasn't going to happen at night as I ran like a maniac hiding from the moon.

My running took me to the least sympathetic man I'd ever met. But even if Jol was the Queen's assassin, he had for some reason kept my secret. He'd never told her that Morland was not my home. He'd never told her that I'd been born on Earth and that by climbing a tree I'd somehow become trapped on his stupid planet.

Morland was the worst.

I knew I wouldn't find the way back. My best chance had probably been when I'd first arrived in Morland five years earlier. I could hardly remember anything about that day. My memories were as misty as a new morning. If I were ever to have found the way home, it would have been right away. Not now when five years of hell had clogged my brain. For the millionth time, I cursed the woods for not showing me the way. The path home had to be out there somewhere. Maybe it was a one-way road that I'd taken. I wondered if I'd even recognize it now. Would I know it if I were face to face with it?

She was coming for me and there was nowhere to hide and nowhere to run and yet hope wouldn't die so I pounded on Jol's door. My hope opened the door a crack and didn't let me in as his glare was somehow casual and yet also piercing.

"There is a warrant on your head, boy. She wants you safe and sound in the castle," he said. "You know what it means coming here to me. Why do you endanger a poor old man?"

"Ha," I barked as I caught my breath. "I'd like to see any of her soldiers just try and take you. I didn't win that bloody competition and become prince with my untutored talent."

"Why are you here, Derek?" Jol asked again. I could see the beginning on flames sparking at his fingertips. Did the Mage really think I was a threat to him?

"I need you to send me home," I said putting pressure on the door. I didn't like being out in the open; the moon could see me.

He sighed letting me in as he flicked his wrist and extinguished the flames. "We've discussed this so many, many times. It is not possible. If you can't find the way you came then I cannot help you," he said in the dismissive exasperation that was his greatest skill.

"Yes, you can," I said coming to tower over him. "There is a way. I heard you that night." The first night Jol had brought me to his home I'd heard him talking to himself after he thought I was asleep and I remembered every word he'd said even if he denied them now.

"Oh, not this again. How many times do I have to tell you that that conversation never happened? It was a dream. If I could send you home, don't you think I would? Don't you think I wouldn't love to be free of you? I assure you that the dream of a Derek-free Morland is the only thing that can send me off to sleep."

"Maybe. Why would you keep this from me otherwise? You said 'it would probably never work'. I remember it crystal clear. That means there is something to try. Something that will only *probably* never work. That's much better than my nonexistent plan which will *definitely* never work."

Seeing that my intimidating pose wasn't working I did the only thing I could think to do. I dropped to my knees and pleaded. "Please, Jol. She's going to kill me tonight. No, it's worse than death. It's worse than anything you could imagine. She's going to give my soul to the Darkness. You've got to get me out of here. I'll do anything!"

"You'd do anything for sure. But would you give anything?"

"I have nothing and I have no one," I said speaking true.

"You'll think that until you hear the price. Whatever your price will be," he said turning around as he rummaged through a large wooden chest at the end of his bed.

"Oh! Then there is a way!" The sheer relief made me stagger for a moment. I had to fight the unnatural urge to hug the old man.

"You will curse me for this one day," Jol said. "I don't know what your price will be but you'll wish I had never mentioned it."

I assured him that I wouldn't. I assured him that anything was better than the living death that was laid out before me. Of course I was wrong. I've never cursed him for it but... the weight of it rests on me constantly. I just wish *I* had been the one to pay the final price.

Jol handed me a small package and explained what I had to do with it. I had no sooner slipped it into my pocket when four guards burst through his door and hauled me back to *her*. They didn't let go of my arms until they forced me into the great hall of the castle. The mirrors to either side played tricks with the mind, making one think it spanned endlessly to the right and left.

Looking into the mirrors a warrior stared back. Morland had made me a deadly tool. My dark red hair was tied back at my neck and my fitted leather armor showed the man I'd become. A thirteen-year-old kid dropped all alone on a nightmare planet became a man very fast. I was now eighteen but I felt ancient. The reflecting mirrors made it look like I'd brought an army of doppelgängers with me but I was alone. The twenty or so real people in the room were soldiers just waiting for their orders. But even with them, the great hall was empty and cold, just like the Queen sitting before me.

Both of her hands rested under her chin and her black hair hung loose behind her. Her relaxed posture did nothing to lessen her harshness. She was only harshness. Sharp edges. Poison dipped thorns. Her intense black eyes held no youth, only death. Her appearance was as much a game as everything else was to her. And I could feel here dark magic roiling beneath her beautiful calm face.

I bowed low kissing the ground and said "Mother." I looked up wondering if I'd even have a chance to try my escape but she nodded her head and the guards took a step back.

"Thank you for extending the courtesy of not executing me on the spot for my rebellion of running away," I said standing.

"Of course, Derek. How could I do that to my favorite son?" she said.

Her only son, I amended to myself. But maybe she didn't know about Gabriel yet.

"What have you decided?" she asked but it wasn't a question and I could see her fingers start to itch as she looked up at the ceiling judging where the moon would be.

"Probably certain death," I said as I took out Jol's present, a red flower, and ate the whole thing in one bite. I said a silent prayer to a god

I knew didn't exist to send me home. As soon as I swallowed the flower I felt it. Strong magic. Dangerous magic.

It felt like... How to describe it? It felt exactly like it should have. Unbearable. It felt like being ripped into a million pieces and then put back together all wrong. I felt my soul being held back and I knew my price. *He* had to stay. I was gone in the blink of an eye hurtling across how many miles, through time and space, to the woods outside of Waxhaw, North Carolina where I'd left five years ago. I could already see houses and cars driving by and the relief that it was all over sent me to my knees.

2

It's been almost five years since I ate that flower and returned home and I still wake up every morning and think for *one moment* that I'm still in Morland. It's a flood of relief when I see my ceiling fan and computer desk and closet full of clothes. But starting my day with Morland on my mind makes the day feel haunted somehow. I then think about Brigitte and I reach for my scar, the scar she gave me that night and it feels like a punch in the stomach when I don't feel it.

Because what I've only alluded to is that all my scars from Morland are gone, well the external ones. I don't have the long scar down my neck from the dog that night Garrison and I went after Julie, or the lash marks on my back from being whipped, or the scar from Brigitte's knife the night I killed her or the many many others. They are all gone, like it all never happened. When I came home from Morland my body was exactly how I'd left it. Thirteen and unmarked. No time had passed on Earth. I don't understand it and I've thought it through to death and still have no answers.

But despite the fact that I have no proof, not even the missing five years, I know it all happened. I feel those five years in my bones and I'm just *so tired*. The quiet and the stillness after so much violence and stress leaves my ears ringing. The other thing that's missing is my soul. When I ate the flower and was brought home, he had to stay.

It's still strange that my soul isn't here. It wasn't strange for him to be on the outside. That had really always felt fine. He was him. I was me. We were the same and not. So it shouldn't make a difference if he's in the other room or if he's on another planet. But it does.

I don't let myself think about him. I don't think about the fact that he is still in Morland or that he's alone with no one who can see him or talk to him. It's too cruel of a cost. I know that I'll never go back to Morland. So we'll never be together again.

At least I know his life is less stressful. He doesn't have me running around jumping from one trap to the next. I hope he's well. I hope I get to be with him when I die. He wouldn't want me to go to Morland to get him and I'm never going back but... I don't know what the future holds. If the past is any indication, then I'm sure it's worse and different than I can imagine.

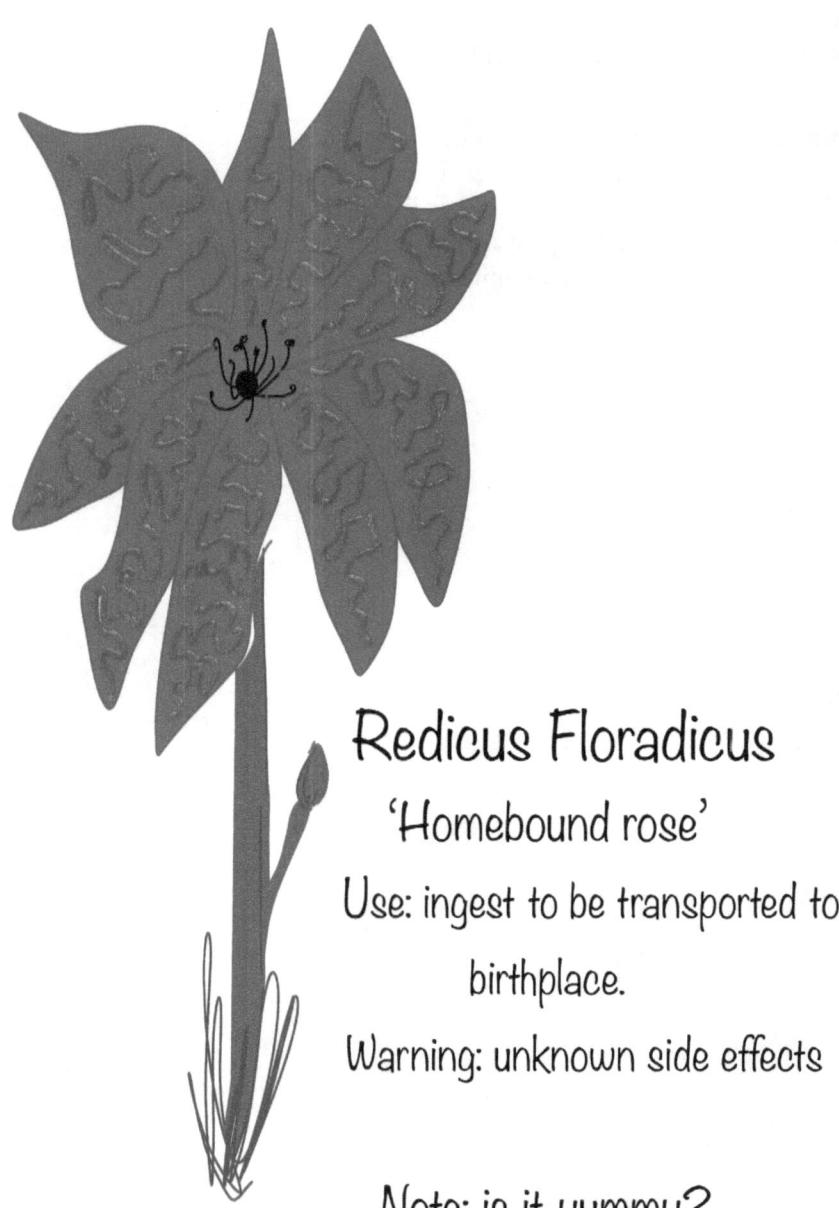

Redicus Floradicus

'Homebound rose'

Use: ingest to be transported to birthplace.

Warning: unknown side effects

Note: is it yummy?

Addendum: Meeting Elinor

1

Things weren't over. But I didn't know that when I wrote that last chapter few years ago. I had no idea what was coming. And her name was Elinor.

We met the first day of the fall semester at Central Piedmont Community College. I didn't know what I was doing there at the Levine campus. It was a favor to my parents and it was *something* to do. I felt like a runner in the starting position just staring at the clock waiting for the timer to start but it just wouldn't. I knew it would but it had been six years since I'd left Morland and I had to do something to fill the time until it started.

We met in the hallway after class. I had noticed her presence as well as everyone else's and she seemed normal to me. I'm usually wrong and this is a perfect example. She was waiting for me and said something like "Hi! Can we talk?" Her cheeks were flushed and her long blonde hair was pulled over one shoulder like she'd been worrying it. I looked her up and down in a quick moment and filed her actions under 'flirtation' and walked away without a word. I had no interest in silly freshmen girls. It was moments like that that made me feel so old. I wasn't nineteen no matter how I looked.

She called after me and wanted to talk more. I sighed and said "Stalker's support group is that way." She looked like a ditsy popular type. If I refused her harshly, word would spread and it would keep her and her posse away. She sputtered something but I was already gone. It was nothing out of the ordinary and I was prepared to forget it... until she was in my next class.

It was just so exactly what I expected from life that I only snickered and rolled my eyes. Thankfully, she was glad to ignore me and I assumed that was it. I tried to forget about her as best I could. But of course, she lived in my neighborhood. I had noticed her checking the mail a few days later and it was almost laughable. But she didn't approach me at school or in the neighborhood and I'd hoped that was the end of it.

But then several weeks later, my best friend, Peter, informed me that a girl would be joining us for our Friday night movie and, of course, her name was Elinor. There could only be the one. I wasn't pleased. That's probably putting it too nicely. I was red-raging. She was ruining everything. Just by existing. She wanted something from me and she was using Peter to get it. Peter is nice, loyal, and has the worst taste in friends. And he's so upsettingly friendly to everyone.

And Elinor had seen this weakness in him and was for some reason trying to worm her way into our friend group. I did not need a complication in my nightmare of a life. It was already too much.

Thankfully, I didn't have to sit by her at the movie but it would have been better if she hadn't sat next to Peter. There had to be a way to separate them and get her back to her own people. Peter already looked a little in love with her. I didn't have the energy to deal with whatever she was because I soon found that she wasn't a normal girl.

I'd assumed that during the movie she would use the time in the dark to cozy up to Peter but instead she seemed to cave in on herself. Like she was trying to become nothing. She closed her eyes and she was... suffering. It was bizarre. When the lights came on she hissed like a monster, put on sunglasses, and then ran to the bathroom. We followed along and after a moment heard the sound of vomiting. Maybe she was bulimic? Or maybe she had a stomach bug or something.

"Sorry," she said when she finally came out of the bathroom, like vomiting was something a person apologized for. "I've got a bad migraine. I need to go home."

Ah that explained it. Of course she'd have 'migraines'. Didn't all women? Wasn't that the most common tool in their arsenal? But I reigned back my internal malice after I scanned her over. She really didn't look well. If she was lying she was a very good actress. Peter agreed to drive Elinor home and I spoke before I thought. "I'll drive her home. She lives five houses down from me." Did that make me look like a stalker? Life was a freakin circle.

I had no idea how drastically this one evening would change my life.

The End

If you enjoyed this book, please leave a review on Goodreads and Amazon.

Reviews mean everything to indie authors like me!

Thank you!

Derek's adventures have only just begun.

Morland isn't done with him yet.

This book series can be enjoyed in two orders.

Magic Headaches > The Morland Prince> Morland Blood

or

The Morland Prince> Magic Headaches> Morland Blood

Here are excerpts of the next books.

Megan Allen

MAGIC
HEADACHES

Elinor just wants her old life. A life before crippling headaches and magic that makes her see another world.

Derek wants to forget his past. A past spent trapped as a prince on another world.

But neither of them gets what they want.

Derek's past is the key to Elinor's future and her magic might be the only thing that can set him free.

That is if they don't kill each other first...

Morland is not a place you go on purpose. Derek spent years trapped on that nightmare of a magic planet and he is never going back. But Elinor's magic headaches are spinning out of control and she needs all the help she can get. She'll even take help from Derek, a soulless murderer with a blog who also happens to be the last born prince of a darkness-wielding fire Queen.

She's doomed. But time is running out. Morland is coming. And Derek will just have to do.

Megan Allen

MORLAND BLOOD

The Darkness is worse than she imagined...

...and just as terrifying as he remembers.

Derek is back on Morland, something he vowed he would never ever do. But sometimes a girl turns a guy into an idiot. Morland is the worst and it has been patiently waiting for him. His mother, the Queen, wants to resume her dark plans that end with a soulless Derek and unimaginable power at her fingertips. But this time is different from the last time Derek was trapped on Morland. This time he isn't alone. He has friends with him. He has Elinor.

Elinor thought her ability to see Morland was a pointless curse but as soon as she stepped onto Morland soil everything changed. Her magic has blossomed into something she doesn't understand and can't control. Danger and Darkness seem to follow their every step as Elinor and her friends try to find some way to free Derek from the Queen's grasp. Despite everything, Peter still thinks Morland is a dream come true while Ryan just wants to survive this nightmare and bring his sister home. When they find a secret group of people hiding from the Queen, Elinor starts training like all of Morland depends on it...which it does. Because the Goodness has been waiting a very long time for a girl like her.

The clock is ticking. The full moon is rising. The Goodness and the Darkness will battle for Derek's soul and the very fate of Morland rests in Elinor's hands. Headaches or no headaches, the task before her seems impossible. Thank the Goodness she isn't alone.

If you enjoyed this book, please leave a review on Goodreads and Amazon.

Megan Allen lives in North Carolina with her husband, daughter, and two giant Ragdoll cats, Poppet and Moxie. She writes books about magic, headaches, and magic headaches. She draws a funny blog about her battle with chronic headaches.

Come find her here:

Website:
MeganAllen.com

Instagram:
Megan_Allen_Author